Unfair Competition

Sophie and Sarah Sandringham had a very ticklish problem on their hands. Two quite different pairs of suitors were demanding those hands in marriage.

The first two persistent gentlemen were among the most elegant to set hearts aflutter with the knot in their cravats and cut of their coats.

The other two were as devoted a pair of childhood sweethearts as ever followed their lady loves from the unspoiled countryside to the sophisticated city.

Clearly, Sophie and Sarah had to put these would-be mates to a test. But first the subtly scheming sisters had to decide whom they wanted to win. . . .

Dilemma
in Duet

———◄•►———

Margaret SeBastian

FAWCETT COVENTRY • NEW YORK

DILEMMA IN DUET

Published by Fawcett Coventry Books, a unit of CBS Publications, the Consumer Publishing Division of CBS Inc.

Copyright © 1979 by Arthur M. Gladstone

All Rights Reserved

ISBN: 0-449-24258-7

Printed in the United States of America

First Fawcett Coventry printing: November 1979

10 9 8 7 6 5 4 3 2 1

Chapter I

————◆●◆————

"This day marches well with my feelings," lugubriously stated the Honorable Percival Deverill as he stood with his hands clasped behind his back and stared out of the sitting room window at the rain dropping steadily from leaden-skies. He turned from the depressing sight and continued: "My dear fellow, I am beginning to have serious doubts that not a one of the Sandringham ladies has entertained a thought of us these past few weeks—in a serious way, if you know what I mean."

Replied Mr. Oliver Grantford from his supine position on a long divan: "Well, Percy, I never did think that you counted for much with them, so I would appreciate your refraining from including me in your plaint regarding Sarah's manner to you."

"Do you tell me you have heard from Sophie?

She has written to you?" asked Percy, all excitement, as he took a step in his friend's direction. "Pray tell me at once! What does she have to say? How is it with them? Do they miss us?"

Oliver shifted his position uncomfortably. "I did not say that I had heard from Sophie. Actually, I do not see the need of it. We have a perfect understanding between us."

"All my eye you do! I suppose this perfect understanding explains why you were as blue as I was when the twins went off to London without bothering to say goodbye to us. Oliver, do not try to come it over me! You and I are in precisely the same boat. You have not heard a word from Sophie and you are just trying to pretend it has not happened."

Oliver frowned. "What has not happened?"

"Oh, don't be so thick, you ass! You are trying to put a good face upon the fact that, as far as the twins are concerned, now that they are gone off to London, *neither* of us counts for a thing with them."

"Really, Percy, you are making too much of it!" snapped Oliver. "It is certainly to be expected that, with all that has occurred, the girls are bound to have their thoughts full of their sister's marriage and to the exclusion of everything else."

"Well, I know that—and I am willing to make all allowance for it—but it is going on seven weeks almost. Surely, in all that time, they could have had one tiny recollection of us, enough to warrant one of them at least sitting down and penning a note saying that they still live."

"Oh, well, you know what they are! I assure you they will get around to it any day now. Just think of all the excitement for them! Their sister is now a countess. Why, all of London must be at their feet. They are quite pretty you know—and with Lord and Lady Dalby to sponsor them, they must be having the time of their lives. I tell you I have half a mind to go down to the city and join in the fun despite what my father says."

"So! You have talked it over with your father! Then you must be as unhappy with the situation as I am."

"The devil you say!"

"Oliver, admit it! You are concerned!" Percy insisted, aggressively.

"Well, of course, I am concerned, but you do not see my crying my eyes out about it, do you?"

"But that is only because you have apartments to let. Pray, what do you think your Sophie will be doing tonight?"

"Oh? Since when have you begun to practice the arts of the gypsies? I haven't the vaguest idea and, what's more, I'll wager neither do you!"

"All right, I do not know what she will be doing, but I am certain that I can tell you what she will not be doing!"

"Prattle on, my boy," returned Oliver with a negligent gesture of his hand.

Percy came over and sat down on the edge of the divan. Looking straight into his friend's face, he said: "Whatever she may be doing, the one thing she will not be doing is to think of you here in Leicestershire, pining away on the edge of Charley Forest."

"I am not pining!"

"You should be! In fact, if you had an ounce of brains, you ought to be more than a little upset. Has it never occurred to you that our twins are about to enter the highest society of the land, that they will be on display at Almack's and the Court? Are you so benighted that you do not know what that must lead to?"

Oliver frowned. "What are you blithering about? They are in no danger, not with the earl and Miss Penelope—er, I mean, Lady Dalby—to look after them."

Percy regarded his friend with disbelieving eyes. Finally he shook his head and said: "Truly, it is unbelievable. I marvel that you were able to finish your studies. My dearest friend, when one comes down to it, you do not have even a trace of wit in that bone box of yours. For God's sake, man, the whole point of their trip into London is to get married!"

"But that's ridiculous! How can they get married when we are here and they are there?" exploded Oliver, indignantly.

"And pray where is it written that they have got to marry us? We are none of us promised to each other."

Oliver had become so distraught that he sat up.

"Percy, I wish you would not say things like that. It is quite upsetting, don't you know."

"Ah, do I detect a glimmer of intelligence? Oliver, it is the usual thing. When ladies, young marriageable ladies of excellent connection, go down to London for their coming out, it is strictly for purposes of matrimony. Now, so long as we loll about here in Woodhouse, we shall not be in the running."

"But that is unthinkable! Sophie would never do such a thing to me!"

"Ah, yes, you have got an understanding between you. Well, I should like to know precisely when you came to it. I know that Sarah and I have no such thing, and it worries me no end. As sisters to a countess, they are fair game for any old duke or marquis that comes along. Neither of us has anything to match such exalted quality."

"Percy, I suspect that you are trying to put me out of humor and I do not thank you for it. But let me assure you, you cannot succeed with me. I know my Sophie. Then, too, you know what they say: Absence makes the heart grow fonder."

"Fonder for whom, dolt? They also say: Out of sight, out of mind—and that sounds to me more appropriate, considering that not a word have we had from either one of them. Why, for all we know, they may already be promised, and we shall be reading about it in the *Gazette* one fine day."

Oliver conferred a very pained look upon his friend. Then he got up and went out into the hall, great purpose in his demeanor. Percy, much puzzled, followed after.

In the hall, Oliver began to put on his cloak and scarf, demanding of Percy: "Well, are you not coming with me?"

"Are you for home?"

"Well, hardly! We have got to do something about all this, don't you think?"

"Indeed we do, but what? Oliver, I am beginning to lose my bearings with you. You have been smugly complacent about the twins' going off to London, while I have been straining all my resources to alert you to the dangers. Now, suddenly, you are all on fire to do something about it, but what, I cannot, for the life of me, comprehend."

By this time Oliver was fully clothed for venturing forth. He paused and looked at his friend with exasperation.

"If you would put that feeble excuse you call a mind to work on the problem, you would understand the jeopardy your love is being threatened with, idiot! It is very possible that neither of the twins realizes that they are promised to us, and I should tremble with misgiving at the prospect of either of them fancy-free and loose in London. We must take steps, I tell you!"

"But, blast you, is not that precisely what I have been at pains to convince you of these last hours?"

"Oh, stop your gab, man! Are you coming or are you not?" demanded Oliver, in a state of high irritation.

"Well, if you have got some idea of how to prevent the unthinkable from occurring, of course— But pray, what do you have in mind to do? Where are we off to?"

"I think it is high time that we had a word with the judge upon the matter. That will at least give us some advantage over the London swells the twins are bound to meet."

Percy looked puzzled. "Oliver, whatever it is that you are using for wits, I am sure you can find something better. We can speak with His Honor until doomsday and it will give us no advantage that I can see."

"It is the simplest thing, my friend. For all the progress any London rake may make with the twins, we shall have gained their parent's permission to broach matrimony with them, whereas they will have to come out to Leicestershire to be able to do as much."

"If I know my Sarah, *that* is not any advantage worth speaking on. In any case, we can make little progress with our loves if they are in London and we are here."

"A matter that is easily remedied. As soon as we have spoken with Mr. Sandringham, we shall go right off to London and settle things with the twins. Then we shall have all of the advantage, don't you see."

"The only thing I see is that we are here and they are there and we had better get cracking— Oh, but I say! How about your father, Oliver? I venture to say he will not be happy about this."

"I shall be having to cause my parent pain, but this is too great a matter to allow of interference even by one's father. Er—how goes it between you and yours?"

"Ripping as always, old chap. You see he does not have to provide for me, as I have a bit of income from my uncle's estate. It makes it quite easy on the governor's pocket not to have to provide for his heir for the nonce."

"Well now, the thing of it is, if my governor is dead set against my going, I shall be hard put for funds. He is not about to underwrite a trip to London for me if his sentiments remain unchanged. Do you think you could advance me a pound or two until—er, until I can pay you back?"

"I suppose I must. It could get rather sticky if I had to go up against both of them all by myself. Oh, blast! We still have not worked out a sure way to tell them apart. I say, do you think we might get some advice upon that score from His Honor? I mean to say, as long as we are to become his sons-in-law, he might as well share the family secrets with us, don't you think?"

"Good God! And pray what do you think he will have to say to us asking for his daughters' hands in marriage and we admit we still have a bit of difficulty distinguishing between them? You keep your mouth shut on that score, my friend, or there will be no point to our traveling to London!"

They came ambling down the road that passed through Woodhouse and went by Bellflower Cottage, the Sandringham residence, located a stone's throw from the gates to Beaumanor, the Earl of Dalby's estate. As they turned into the Sandringham's walk, they began to straighten their clothing and smooth their hair. Then, very erect and feeling exceedingly mature, they came up to the cottage door.

"Do I look all right?" asked Oliver as he raised his hand to the knocker.

"Oh, do get on with it! One would think this is our first visit. It is only Judge Sandringham we have come to speak with, and you know he is no stickler for ceremony."

"Yes, well—" And he knocked upon the door.

It opened and a pert serving girl answered it.

"Ah, Mr. Oliver and Mr. Percy!" she said and smiled up at them.

"My dear Tessie, we have come to hold conversation with His Honor. There's a girl! Do you inform the judge we are calling."

She cocked her head and brought her first finger up to the side of her cheek. "Oh, but I do not have the fare, my fine gentlemen. And I am blessed if I could get to him on foot."

"Ah, I take it that His Honor is out," said Percy. "When do you expect him back?"

"He never condescended to inform me of his plans, you see. I would venture to suggest it might be a sennight—but it could as easily be for a fortnight."

"Oh, well, if he is gone on circuit, we should be delighted to speak with Mrs. Sandringham."

"Then you shall have to find your way to London, sirs, for that is where she has gone to be with our countess."

"Oh, blast!" exclaimed Percy. "Well then, pray inform us as to the most likely place we might locate His Honor. You see, we must have a chat with the gentleman. It is of the most urgent."

"Then you shall have to go down to the city, for that is where he is—with the missus and his daughters. There be no one about here."

The two gentlemen exchanged stricken glances.

"Great Jupiter!" exclaimed Oliver. "It is all over for us then!"

"Thank you, Tessie! Good day," said Percy as he grabbed Oliver by the elbow and drew him away out to the road.

Before he let him go, he gave his arm a shake and exclaimed: "Man, are you out of your mind? Must you run off at the mouth before a servant? Now it will be all over the shire that we are in some sort of trouble! What will people think?"

"I don't give a bloody damn what anyone thinks! Do you not realize what this means? We are trepanned, I tell you! We have lost our chance! What with the entire family gone off to London, we are helpless to vie for our loves!"

"We are not helpless—and, furthermore, I cannot believe that the twins, whom we have known all our lives, have forgotten us. But we certainly shall lose our chance with them if we continue to stand about and debate the point."

"But, Percy, think on it a moment, I pray. Here,

the entire family has gone off to London and never a word to us. I mean to say, how comes it that we did not know of it—?"

"Because we were occupied and intensely so, or have you forgotten? Indeed, such application as you showed these past days at school was most remarkable. Considering how miserably you have done in the past, I must say you managed to finish it in a burst of glory—for you, that is."

Oliver grinned. "Thank you, old chap. I did manage to put it over on my governor, didn't I. I will admit he had me in a bit of a sweat—tore great strips out of my hide when it appeared I should fail the blasted chase. Didn't think I could do it."

"Neither did I—but we both had our hands full what with cracking books and burning the midnight oil—"

"Bah! It just shows what comes of all of this bloody learning! Now our heads are swollen with a bunch of stuffy nonsense and we are in a way to losing the lights of our lives!"

"At least school for us is over and we are free to pursue our desires—and that is precisely what I am about to do. I am off for London. I fear I have got quite a bit to make up. It is one thing for us to have forgotten everything in order to finish the term, but I am blessed if I can understand how comes it that Sarah had no word at all for me before she left. I am for London to demand an explanation!"

"And I, too!" vehemently agreed Oliver. "I say, old chap, you have not forgotten that I am short of the ready and will need a spot of help from you, have you?"

"Of course I have not—but I shall in a minute if you do not crack on speed. I am not about to spend another day mooning about. There is the evening mail for London out of Leicester and I expect to be on it tonight—and you had better be on it with me if you know what is good for you!"

Chapter II

◆—◆◆

The Temple, that is no more London than it is Westminster, was no proper place for an earl to have his residence. That was the considered opinion of Miss Sophie and Miss Sarah Sandringham. From the moment they stepped into the rooms that their brother-in-law Lord Dalby had let temporarily, they were sure that their stay in London was not going to be the great fun that they had anticipated. And now, after more weeks than they cared to count, their worst fears were being realized, day after dreary day.

The two young ladies were seated in the bed-sitting room they shared, close to a window from which they could observe the comings and the goings along King's Bench Walk. This particular pastime was proving to be the most excitement they could enjoy the past few days.

Said Sophie: "It isn't as though he is a real earl, you know."

"Well, he is better than no earl at all, don't you think?"

"I dare say—but why could not he have been an earl all his life instead of coming into the title so late in life?"

Sarah grinned. "I imagine that Alan would have preferred it that way, too. The thing that is so bad is the business of the law. I could have wished that Pennie had had better taste as far as vocation is concerned. I mean to say, what with our father a judge, one would have thought that Pennie would have had all the law she could stand. Now, here is Alan going off to become a judge, too! There's the trouble! Had he been an earl's son, like any other reasonable earl, he'd never have had to go in for the law."

"Well, but now that he is an earl and wed, one would think he'd have more important things to think about than the law! I mean to say, it is a positive shame that we should all of us come to London just so that Alan can become a judge. I do declare that the city is much too good a place to waste upon something so inconsequential."

"And, pray, what of our sister? Can you imagine any countess so senseless as to hang about the law courts all day? I am sure if Penny had been born a countess she'd never *think* of doing anything so silly."

"Yes, but then Papa would have been an earl, and it would have been nothing at all for Pennie to have wed one," said Sophie with a chuckle. "I prefer it this way—and, after all, Alan is not at all a bad sort for a brother-in-law."

"If only he would receive his appointment to the Bench so that we can get on with the important matters."

"Mama says that it will not be long now and we must be patient."

"Well, that is easy enough for her to say! She has Papa and, anyway, she is long past parties and dances, whereas we are just beginning," protested Sarah. "And Pennie has Alan, and she, too, is years in advance of us. I do declare, it is a pitiable thing to be the youngest in the family."

"Well I am even younger than you, sister dear," stated Sophie.

"I am sure that a difference of twenty minutes in age is not to be reckoned. The fact is we both of us share in the distinction. My advanced minutes do not change the case for me a farthing's worth. Really, instead of sitting about, why do we not go out by ourselves?"

"Because unmarried females, especially young ones, cannot do so in London. It is considered very fast—though I do not see why."

"Nor I. It is nothing like that in Leicestershire. I almost wish we were back home. At least we could be out and doing. I never thought that London could be so stuffy. But look you, Sophie! See out on the walk? There is a lady going about by herself, and I am sure she is not more than a year or two our senior. If she can go about by herself, I do not see why we cannot. At least there are the two of us to see after each other. I do not see any harm in it."

Sophie was studying the lady as she went strolling by. "Those gentlemen seem to be much taken with her. See, they have stopped to look after her. Is that so very bad? Everyone in Leicester and even Nottingham always looked after *us*, and no one took exception to it. Just because this is London is no reason for things to be all that different. I think we should go out. We shan't be gone long. We can stroll about the walk and perhaps a little farther and come right back. In fact, if we are awfully quiet about it, even the servants will not know we are out—and we shall be back well before Mama and Pennie return from Lady Carr's."

Sarah had not the least intention of offering any objection; so that no debate ensued. The girls rose as one, and went to their wardrobe and selected their wraps. It was November without, and London was enjoying a spot of damp and chilly weather.

Peering carefully out of their room to make sure there was no one to see them depart, they slipped out into the hall and, quietly as mice, eased open the door to the apartment. Closing it silently, they tiptoed down to the street floor and exited onto King's Bench Walk. Neither had to caution the other to stay close to the buildings lest they be seen from the apartment, and they walked briskly along for a bit until they were sure that they had made their escape unobserved.

The little group of gentlemen was still assembled, each member of which was standing by or leaning against the railing, engaging in aimless conversation. But their talk stopped when the two young ladies appeared, and they proceeded to stare at their receding figures, blinking their eyes in puzzlement. One of them even rubbed his eyes and looked again. Finally he shook his head and exclaimed: "I say, did you see what I thought I saw?"

"Really, Blessingame, a bit of a fuss to raise over a pair of females, don't you think?"

"Then there were two of them, were there?"

"What, do I have to tally the score for you? Of course there were two of them. See? They haven't turned the corner yet. Count 'em! One—two—and I will admit they are a rather neat pair from what I can see of 'em."

"Ah, then you did not see their faces, I take it."

"No, they turned away too quickly. What did they look like?"

"Now that is the most incredible thing!"

"I wasn't looking in their direction when they came out. Still I do not see the least thing incredible about it!" snapped Lord Fallon.

"No, Frank, I wasn't speaking about that! Their faces, man! It is unbelievable!"

"A pair of beasts, eh?"

"A pair of angels rather! But the thing of it is, if I can believe my own eyes, they have got the same face between them."

Lord Fallon regarded Lord Blessingame with

suspicion. "Are you bosky, old man? They have got two heads—I mean, they each have a head—and so I must assume, they have each got a face—"

"No, imbecile! There are two faces, but they are the same. I tell you, they are twins and adorable!"

"But what business can they have in the Inner Temple? They are neither barristers nor solicitors nor benchers—they are females!"

"Why, bless you, you noticed!" laughed Lord Blessingame. "Now I would suggest that instead of indulging ourselves in dry speculation, we go after the little dears and learn from their pretty lips precisely their business in the Temple. What do you say, Frank?"

"I say, time is fleeting!" exclaimed Lord Fallon, launching himself from the railing.

As the two gentlemen proceeded quickly along the walk Lord Blessingame remarked: "Are you acquainted with any one residing at No. 6? I suspect that we shall have to find an introduction to the place somehow. By heaven, if those two are the sort of company these legal chaps keep, there is a deal more to be said for the profession than I thought!"

Sarah and Sophie strolled along Tudor Street in the belief that they would come shortly to the Temple Gardens, but they were quite turned around and, upon entering Salisbury Square, were sure they were not headed in the proper direction. They came to a stop and began to discuss what they ought to do.

"We ought to have come to the gardens by this time," remarked Sarah.

"Well, we have not. I suggest that we go back the way we came and try again."

"Oh, I say! Those two gentlemen we passed on the walk are right behind us. Do we dare make inquiry of them?"

Sophie frowned. "I suppose we could, but if we are doing something exceptional by going about unescorted, that might be even more so."

"The thing is, when it is discovered, we shall be in a nice kettle of fish, and so I say what of it?"

"And so say I!"

With one accord, the two ladies turned and began to walk toward the gentlemen, who immediately stopped and engaged themselves in conversation while they waited for the two girls to pass. To their amazement, the twins came up to them and began to speak.

"Sirs, we are a bit confused in our direction. Would you be kind enough to direct us to Temple Gardens?"

For a moment, both gentlemen were too stunned to respond. Although they could not have wished for a better beginning, it was completely unlooked for, and they needed time to reorder their notions.

Lord Fallon was the first to recover. He bowed and said: "Indeed, ladies, it would be our pleasure to escort you to the gardens. It is not so very far. I am your servant, Frank Fallon."

"Indeed, it would be a delight to show you the

way, ladies," added Lord Blessingame. "Your servant, ladies, Jack Blessingame."

"It is most kind of you. We are the Misses Sandringham."

They split up into two couples and began to stroll back, the two gentlemen still a little dazed and very much puzzled. It had been so easy one was forced to conclude that this lovely pair was fast, yet they had the manner of ladies. It left the two gentlemen in confusion and unable to decide how to treat them.

Finally Lord Blessingame had a brilliant idea. He said to Sarah: "You have not been in London long?"

"No, just a matter of weeks, and things have been at sixes and sevens all that time, so we have had little chance to go out. Have you been in London long?"

But His Lordship had turned back to address Lord Fallon. "They have not been in London long."

"So Miss Sandringham has informed me. I think it is incumbent on us to show the ladies the town."

"A most excellent idea!" He turned to Sarah. "Where are you staying? I shall come for you this evening."

"Oh, but I do not think that that would be at all proper. After all we are not truly acquainted. Would it not be better if you were to pay a call some morning, or isn't that the way things are done in the city?"

"Oh, well, yes, if you would prefer it. It is just

that I thought— Well, never mind what I thought. I shall make it my business to visit tomorrow morning, if that is all right with you."

"I should be very pleased to see you, but—oh dear, I suppose it would be too soon. You see, the way things are the earl is never about when he is needed and the countess is forever away with him, and then, Mama and Papa are staying with Aunt Claudia, our only London relation; so you see it will be quite difficult to arrange for any one to receive you on a moment's notice."

Feeling suddenly like a man in imminent danger of drowning, Lord Blessingame murmured: "Earl? Countess? I—I am not sure I understand, Miss Sandringham—or is it Lady Sandringham, perhaps?"

"No, no, just plain Miss Sandringham. It is my sister who is the lady, you see. She is Countess Dalby which, of course, makes Allan, the Earl of Dalby, my brother-in-law. In fact, if I have not made it clear, my sister and I are staying with them."

Lord Blessingame blinked. "You are the sister of a countess and have been in London some weeks? My dear Miss Sandringham, I am at a loss to credit this. How comes it that I find you immured away in the Temple and have never seen you at any function? Had you appeared at any one of them, you and your sister must have become the talk of the town—and its toast, I do not hesitate to add. Are you engaged in some litigation that we discovered you on these grounds?"

"Why, no, not at all. You see the Earl of Dalby is

a man of law, a sergeant, in fact, so it is only natural that he should bring his wife to the Temple, his only residence in London, until he has made arrangements to remove to a proper house. Since he cannot entertain until that is accomplished, it is his first order of business to provide a proper London establishment. Unfortunately, there is also the business of his appointment to the Bench: so between the two businesses nothing much is being accomplished, and we have got to be patient until all is arranged."

"You mean to say that you are *residing* at No. 6, King's Bench Walk?"

Sarah regarded him with a doubtful smile. "Mr. Blessingame, is there some reason for you to doubt what I have said?"

"My dear Miss Sandringham, to say I doubt your word is putting it a little strong. I am just having the least bit of difficulty swallowing it all at one gulp. Pray inform me as to your father. I imagine that he is something in a special way, too."

"Indeed! He is an eminent juror on the Leicestershire Circuit."

"Yes—it had to be something like that. And I am sure he is in the habit of allowing his daughters to roam about the city, completely unprotected, liable to be saluted by the most offensive riffraff. My dear Miss Sandringham, what do you take me for? It is obvious to me that you are from the country, Leicestershire, no doubt. That much I am willing to credit, but I warn you to get a bit of town bronzing before you try to work your wiles upon me!"

For a moment Sarah was quite still. She stopped in her tracks and regarded him with distaste. Then, as Sophie and Lord Fallon came up, she remarked: "Sophie, we have been misguided. We were under the impression that we were speaking with gentlemen, but this creature informs me that we are entertaining offensive riffraff."

"What the devil!" exclaimed Lord Fallon. "Jack, what is the meaning of this?" he demanded angrily.

"I fear Miss Sandringham has quite misunderstood my remark. I said that it is incredible that with the connections she pretends to, she would be permitted to roam the streets unescorted."

"Pretends to? If I do not find incredible my Miss Sandringham's connections, I do not see how you can find them exceptional. I believe you have insulted the lady and I demand that you apologize at once."

"Frank, have you lost your wits? I admit two such perfect beauties can bereave a man of his common sense but, fortunately, I am able to look beyond appearances."

"Then, I declare this once you have looked too far. Desford is going to be quite unhappy with you. If he demands an apology from you, I venture to say you will have a devil of a time refusing him."

"Desford? How in blazes does he come into it?"

"Well, what in God's name have you been discussing all this while? Surely Miss Sandringham has informed you of the connection."

"She never mentioned Desford. She is full up with earls and countesses. Now I am fairly well acquainted with my fellow peers hereabouts and I am sure I have never heard of an Earl of Dalby."

"Dalby and Desford are one and the same, imbecile! *That* was the business he left town for some months ago. It all fits. We knew he had gone out to see to this windfall of an inheritance. Apparently he has done it up brown. From barrister to earl." Lord Fallon grinned. "Rather peculiar, isn't it, to discover that one's barrister suddenly takes precedence over one?"

"Why the nerve of the fellow! But he was a mere commoner!"

Sarah turned to Sophie and said? "Sister, I have had enough air for today. Let us return home. I imagine we shall get the devil for this little escapade."

Sophie turned to Lord Fallon. "My lord, it was most pleasant to make your acquaintance. I hope we shall be seeing more of you."

"Indeed, you shall Miss Sophie. I have an acquaintance with Alan Desford and I am bound to look in on him and offer my congratulations on his good fortune—not to say how curious I am to meet his new countess."

Lord Blessingame was staring shamefacedly at Sarah. "My dear Miss Sandringham, what can I say?"

"Lord Blessingame, you have said too much already. Come, Sophie."

Lord Fallon kissed Sophie's hand in fond farewell, while Lord Blessingame with features flushed could only nod.

Chapter III

———◦———

When the twins ascended up to the first floor of No. 6, they discovered the little household to be in a high state of excitement and worry. A maid immediately informed them that Her Ladyship was in bad humor over their disappearance and was upon the verge of calling upon the constabulary. They had better go to her immediately.

They discovered their sister in the small parlor walking about the room in a state of distraction which turned to anger immediately upon their entrance.

"So there you are!" cried Lady Penelope. "What, are you trying to pluck the heart out of me? How dare you to leave the premises without a word to anyone—and without an escort? You are not at home in Woodhouse! This is London, and young ladies never, but never, go about the streets by themselves. What will people think?"

"I do not care a fig what people think!" declared Sophie. "And just because you are become a countess, Pennie, is no reason for you to put on airs with us!"

"I am your older sister and you are in my charge, Sophie. It is no different here than it was at home. I always stand in for Mama when she is not present—and do not think that things have changed just because I am occupied at the moment."

"Well, I do not see what all the fuss is about. We merely went for a stroll is all. Surely there is nothing exceptional in that."

"It could be more than exceptional. An unescorted female, especially young, could be approached by all manner of unsavory characters, and I assure you, London is filled with them."

"Well, we did not meet up with anyone like that—"

"Speak for yourself!" cried Sarah. "I met with a most unpleasant sort and, as far as I am concerned, I would just as soon be back in Leicestershire if that is what goes for a gentleman in London!"

Sophie turned on her sister. "I *thought* something was awry with you two. I can't imagine what. Frank and I got along famously."

"Frank!" exclaimed Lady Penelope in high indignation. "Do you tell me that you spoke with someone without you were properly introduced? Sophie, how very brazen of you! Now you know that that is not even a proper way to go even at home!"

"Truly, Pennie, it was nothing so bad as you make out. Frank did not seem to mind. In fact he proposes to come calling. Then the proper introductions can be made. I do not see that there is any need to make a fuss."

"If he is anything like his friend, Lord Blessingame, then I say there is!" countered Sarah. "I do not think you understand what they took us for. Pennie is right. We should not have gone out by ourselves. London is a horrid place."

"Lord Blessingame? Is that what he told you?" inquired Lady Penelope with a frown.

"Come to think of it he did not. But that is how the gentlemen addressed each other—"

"They are Lord Fallon and Lord Blessingame," volunteered Sophie. "It is no wonder you are not pleased with your gentleman if he had not the manners to introduce himself to you."

"The thing of it was that he did not credit anything I said," retorted Sarah. "So you can just imagine what he must have been thinking of us. I assure you, I never felt so insulted in all my life!"

"Well, that is what comes of young ladies going about town without a proper escort," declared Lady Penelope very firmly, "and this had better be the very last time it occurs or I shall pack you off to Leicestershire with Mama and Papa when they leave."

"They can leave right this instant for my part," retorted Sarah. "There is not a blessed thing for us to do on any count, and when we do go out for a venture, it is perfectly horrid. I do not like London one bit!"

"But, Sarah, all of the gentlemen in London cannot be as bad as Lord Blessingame. I do assure you that Frank is most gallant and nothing at all exceptional," argued Sophie. "I should be quite lonely here without you. We have never been separated before."

Concern filled Lady Penelope's eyes. Her younger sisters were like one, always together in whatever they did, even at their most mischievous. The idea of their parting was unthinkable.

She said: "I am sure there is no need for anything so drastic. I have just come from the broker and I believe we have found a house. Once we are moved into it, things will be different, I promise you. We have not been able to entertain here in these cramped quarters and so it has been very trying for you. I beg you will be patient for but a fortnight and then you shall see how much fun London can be. Alan and I intend to maintain a household quite fitting for an earl, and he is as enthusiastic as I am to see the pair of you properly launched into the fashionable world. Sarah, by the time the new season begins, you will see that there will be more to do than you have time for."

"For more of the Blessingame sort I would not spare a second of time. Truly, Sophie, you are not being at all sensible. This Lord Fallon cannot be all that much if he will condescend to speak with strange females he encounters in the street. When

you come to consider it calmly, Lord Blessingame
was in his rights to question our respectability.
Then, too, there is the fact of the gentlemen's
veracity. How do we know that they are in truth
lords—or even gentlemen for that matter?"

Lady Penelope's lips twitched, but she said
nothing, waiting for Sophie to respond.

She did.

Said Sophie: "Oh, one can tell that they were
gentlemen, even if there was something distasteful
in Lord Blessingame's manner to you. As for their
being of the nobility, well, I do not know about
Lord Blessingame, but I am willing to swear Lord
Fallon is a peer at least. Such gentle manners and
gallant speaking could only be that of a noble."

Sarah glared at her twin.

"Now, now, my pets," intervened Lady Penelope, "it hardly matters what the station of these
strangers are. I have a feeling you will not be
seeing them again. I am inclined to agree with
Sarah that, if they were proper gentlemen, they
would not have addressed themselves to you without an introduction. I say it is just as well that you
did not remain longer with them—"

"But they cannot be strangers, Pennie," Sophie
broke in. "I distinctly heard them refer to Alan. In
fact, I understood Lord Blessingame to have had
legal business with him. Wait till my lord returns
and he can vouch for them. You heard them,
Sarah."

Sarah nodded. "It is so, Pennie, but it makes no

difference to me. If, perchance, Lord Blessingame should deign to call, I shall not be in to him."

"Well, be that as it may, we shall all of us talk it over with Alan when he comes. In the meantime, I was thinking that you might like to see the house we have selected. I warn you it is a sight larger than Bellflower Cottage but never so great as Beaumanor. There are all sorts of chambers in it, and Alan has said that you each may choose your own."

At once both twins' eyes lit up, and they were all enthusiasm to go out at once.

"Well, first we had better have a bite to eat, for it is still hours before dinner, and I shall tell you all about it while we eat."

Lady Penelope was relieved to see how easily Sophie and Sarah were diverted from what threatened to be a heated dispute. She could not recall a time when either of her sisters had exhibited animosity for the other, and it had been quite a shock to her to hear Sarah give expression to a rare difference of opinion with Sophie and do so with animosity. It was quite shaking and she fervently hoped that it would never occur again. She, and all the rest of the family, was used to thinking of the twins as a sort of composite person and rarely making any distinction in her treatment of either of them. Silently she hoped that neither Lord Fallon nor Lord Blessingame would bother to put in an appearance but had little faith her wish would be granted if they were already in the acquaintance of her husband, the earl.

As they proceeded toward the little dining room and the twins began to belabor her with questions about the new Desford residence, she began to think that it was the confinement that the twins had undergone that had led to the falling out, even as it had brought them into the mischief of leaving the apartment without a proper escort. She parried their questions with a laugh, and the air felt much lighter.

They took their seats about the table, and as a light luncheon was served, she hushed them and said: "All right, you two! If you promise not to dawdle over your food, I shall tell you about the place, and then we can go out to visit it.

"Alan had a wish to see us settled in Mayfair, which is the very best address in London, but when I heard what prices were being asked, it went against the grain with me. His Honor-to-be, my Lord Earl of Dalby, has no need for such extravagance. His station, coupled with his seat upon the Bench, will speak sufficiently to his eminence, and so we settled for a most excellent house in Cavendish Square. Actually it is *practically* in Mayfair, it being but a block beyond Oxford Street, which is said to be the unofficial boundary, you see. So, while we might not be housed in the very epitome of fashion yet, it is an ample house, I do assure you, and not squeezed in between its neighbors. It is in fact something of a mansion, I should say, what is called a townhouse, and I doubt that anyone will have the temerity of looking down upon us for having selected it. The thing is it has a fine ballroom, and neither Alan nor I are adverse to a bit of entertainment every now and again."

"It sounds perfectly marvelous to me," said Sarah. "But what of our neighbors there?"

"A very excellent sort of people, quite unexceptional in every respect. I know for sure that there is a wealthy marquis living on the square in season."

"Is he handsome?" asked Sophie.

"I truly do not know, but I imagine his marchioness must think so," said Lady Penelope with a little laugh. "Oh, but do not be in a rush to set your caps, my dears. You have got a great many people to meet and a great many places to visit. I tell you, life in the city is just beginning for you— as it is for me, too. I know precisely how bad you have been feeling, all confined as you have been, and I marvel that you did not get yourselves into some mischief sooner and I am pleased with your forbearance. But you see it could not be helped. Alan and I had a wish to be by ourselves after the wedding and only gave thought to where we would reside—er, well, it was quite a bit later—but, by that time, I, unthinkingly, had had the strongest wish for a sight of my baby sisters and had sent for you. I never expected Mama and Papa to come, too, and that is why we have had to put them up with Aunt Claudia. Now, just as we shall be putting everything together, they will be leaving us, for Papa has his court duties to pursue and he has got to get ready for the Sessions back home."

"Oh pray, Pennie, we shall not have to go back with them, shall we?" pleaded Sarah. "It would be such a dreadful waste to have come all the way to London and have naught worthwhile to remember."

Maintaining a look of great sobriety, Lady Penelope assured her sister that it had been arranged for the twins to stay with Lord and Lady Dalby for the entire season.

"But, my dears, now that I am a countess, I shall not be able to keep my eyes on you all the time: therefore, Aunt Claudia has kindly consented to come live with us. She will look after you."

"I do not think I recall Aunt Claudia. What is she like?"

"Well, you will be seeing her before very long. We shall be having her over for dinner one evening soon—and Mama and Papa, too. But you were very young when she came out to Leicestershire that once. I can tell you she will not stand for any nonsense—"

The twins made a face.

"But that is not to say she is not a dear person—and what is more, she knows everything that is worth knowing about the fashionable world, so you will be well advised to be guided by her. I had the pleasure of staying with her a full season many years back and, frankly, I enjoyed her company more than anyone else's whom I encountered that miserable time."

"We'd so much rather have you, Pennie," said Sarah.

"Yes, my loves, and I hope that it will always be so, but now, I must think of Alan, you know."

"If I did not like him so much, I think I should hate him for having taken you away from us."

"You speak like a child! He has not taken me away from you. Actually, he loves you both dearly and never objected when I asked if you might come to me. So I pray you will continue to love him, too."

"Well, it is not a particularly hard thing to do. So I daresay we shall, won't we, Sophie?"

"I think we had better. Papa excepted, he is the only man who ever caught us out."

Feigning a look of worry, Lady Penelope remarked: "Well, I pray that somewhere in England there exists at least two other gentlemen blessed with that particular talent."

Chapter IV

———◆———

As the hackney drew in to the curb, the eager look of anticipation that was mirrored on the twins' faces faded rapidly. Sarah turned to her Ladyship and asked: "Is this it?"

"Yes, love, this is Cavendish Square. How do you like it?"

"Not at all. It is no whit better than the Temple. Oh, Pennie, there is barely room to breathe!"

"If you will be pleased to step outside, you will see that that remark is not quite accurate. Of course, I know it does not bear comparison to the forests and the fields of home, but believe me, for London, it is one of the few places one can see so much of the sky."

Sarah and Sophie descended from the carriage as though it were a chore, and their sister came out after them, turning to the cabbie to whom she gave instruction to await them.

In the meantime, the twins stood upon the sidewalk and stared about them. The building before which they stood was a huge, three-story, overpowering pile standing as one of a quartet of similar edifices along one edge of the square, each separated from the other by a single-story structure of undistinguished appearance, all of them attached. They resembled a gargantuan tessellated parapet, with the much smaller buildings, lining the other sides of the square, their outerworks. The square itself was mostly cobbled except for a great circular portion in its center. Here grass was planted and a circular walk inlaid, the whole surrounded by an iron railing which appeared to keep all the world out, for the gate, if there was one, was particularly hard to distinguish from the rest of the enclosing ironwork.

Sophie and Sarah, used, as they were, to the spaciousness of Leicestershire, were not at all happy with the prospect and stared glumly about them. To their eyes, even the buildings lacked all pretense to charm. They were too high for the lack of space which surrounded them and they appeared to be, each in its grouping, very like each other. They were used to cottages and manor houses set in green expanses of well-tended lawns on one hand and, on the other, the wild scenery where Charnwood Forest threatened to rush down from its hills and engulf the vales. This Cavendish

Square was very little better than the confines of the Temple.

Lady Penelope sighed and remarked: "Truly, my dears, it is nothing like home, but it is a deal better than anything else we saw. I pray you will make the best of it. After all, it is not as if you have got to live in it forever. Just think—"

She was interrupted by an old but hearty-looking fellow issuing forth from the great townhouse. He was in his shirtsleeves and wore a leathern apron. He came toward them, his mouth wide with a welcoming grin, his hands clasped together before his chest, ducking his head.

"Oh, for heaven's sake!" exclaimed Her Ladyship.

"Jepperson!!" shrieked the twins, and they rushed forward to greet the old retainer of the earl's. "When did you leave Beaumanor?"

"Indeed, Jepperson, when did you—and whatever for?" queried Her Ladyship with a puzzled frown.

The old man straightened up, and the smile faded from his lips as he regarded the countess with some concern. "I pray Your Ladyship is not put out of countenance by my appearance. His Lordship thought it might be a pleasant surprise, Your Ladyship, for you to see a familiar face in this new place."

Lady Penelope reached out and touched his hand. "Dear Jepperson, indeed, I am overwhelmed with pleasure that you should tear yourself away from Beaumanor to come to the city. My only concern is that you might feel uncomfortable so far away from all that pertains to the chase. I would just adore to have you for butler in this my first establishment."

Jepperson bowed. "Thank you, Your Ladyship. I am so relieved to hear it. I could not be sure but that you might have preferred a younger more knowledgeable man for the post. I must admit the ways of these London people are a sight different from what I was used to back on the estate. They are something cheeky, don't you know, Your Ladyship."

"Oh, I am sure that you can handle them properly enough—but I still do not understand how you come to be here. We only came to a decision about the house this morning."

"I hope I do not speak out of turn when I inform Your Ladyship that His Lordship requested my presence in London some days ago on purpose to hold myself in readiness against the time a residence should be decided upon."

"Well, I am certainly surprised and pleasantly so. Have you seen His Lordship recently?"

"But seconds ago, Your Ladyship. He is within at this moment and having the devil's own time with the arrangements—if you will pardon my saying so, Your Ladyship. The furniture and the furnishings that come with the place—well, I must say that my experience with Beaumanor in no way qualifies me for such decisions. I fear that nothing in His Lordship's experience qualifies him either."

"Well now, this is carrying a good thing a bit far,

I must say. I'll thank His Lordship to restrain himself. Come, do you lead me to the earl. It is neither fitting nor proper that he concern himself with the furnishings. I shall see to that. We both know at what a loss he was trying to make Beaumanor fit for company. Why he should think he can do better here, I swear I do not know. Come, Jepperson, take me to your master. I never intended that we should do ought but store the stuffs that clutter up this house. We have got to start afresh," she said as she and the twins began to follow Jepperson inside. She turned to her sisters and continued: "Sophie! Sarah! I pray you will not pull long faces for Alan to see. He is particularly proud of this house for the reason that it is the first place he has chosen for his own rather than inherited. I must warn you that it is no Bellflower Cottage you are entering. It is dark and dreary by comparison, but once we have got it refurbished properly, I assure you it will be quite pleasant."

"Surely, sister dear, we are well enough bred to act the lady with our brother-in-law," responded Sophie.

"And it will be a welcome change from the confines of the Temple, too," added Sarah. "May we help you decide in the decoration."

"I have every intention of allowing it, loves. I can hardly do it all by myself. Pray, what are little sisters for?"

They followed Jepperson into the house and discovered a flurry of activity. Apparently the earl had been busy indeed. There was a strange set of ser-

vants going about with dust rags and polish, and
when they came into the grand drawing room, they
discovered the earl standing in the center of the
room, looking quite distracted as he pondered the
arrangement of the various pieces of furniture scat-
tered about the chamber in a most disorganized
fashion.

"My lord, it will never do. None of it," remarked
Lady Penelope.

At the sound of her voice, the earl wheeled
about and came to her with a great smile. "Ah,
Pennie, you could not have come at a better time.
I had hoped to have it all done for you, but I am
defeated. You are so right. Nothing appears to
fit—and how do my new sisters find this, the new
residence of Lord and Lady Dalby, eh?"

"Oh, it is much improved over the Temple," said
Sophie.

"Sophie Sandringham!" exclaimed Lady Penelope.

The earl laughed. "If that is the best you can
say for it, then I commission you to bring it up to
snuff. Heaven knows I cannot."

"Alan, indeed it was awfully sweet of you to try,
and I thank you for it, sweetheart, but why do you
not retire from the field and let me take over for
you? And incidentally, grant me carte blanche, for
we shall have to have all new things. What we
have here may have been in the latest style for
King Alfred, but times have changed, my dear, and
with them tastes as well."

"I suspect it will be fearfully expensive."

"For Barrister Desford, yes, but never for the Earl of Dalby."

He turned to the twins. "That sister of yours has turned mercenary of a sudden—or is it a defect in her character I missed?"

"Good heavens, Alan, as long as I was going to marry an earl, what a fool I should have been to wed a poor one," retorted Lady Penelope.

He grinned and replied: "Now, how does it come out if I were to apply the same reasoning to my selection of a countess?"

"Ah," said Sophie, "but then you would have not have had us for your relations, my lord."

"Egad, you are right! I shall sue for a divorce in the morning."

Lady Penelope nodded smilingly and replied: "Yes, you do that, my lord. At least it will take you from here and allow me to put this place in order. Oh, by the way, dearest, what is new with regard to your appointment?"

"You may find this incredible, my love, but they are having a bit of difficulty with the fact that I am an earl. There is going to be an opening in the Court of King's Bench, which is precisely the appointment I would have preferred; but, since one is supposed to be knighted upon that elevation, what does one do with an earl? Apparently it is not a situation that has come up too often and until the nice points of protocol are settled, the patent will not issue. Lord Ellenborough, I am pleased to say, is furious, as is your father, and I do not think the Master of the Rolls, who is the chief protester, will be able to stand up against those two. Pennie, you can be very proud of your father. Considering he is but a circuit judge, it gave me the deepest feeling of pride to see the Lord Chief Justice give attentive ear to all he had to say. That is quite a father-in-law I gained."

"Well, my lord, I sincerely hope it is something more than an eminent father-in-law you had in mind when you married me."

"I suspect that there might have been, my sweet. Well now, I do believe, having done my best here, it is time to take my leave. After what you did for Beaumanor, I have every reason to expect you can do as much for the Desford residence. Do you think you will have it ready for us to move into it by the week's end?"

Lady Penelope gasped and then she burst into laughter. "My dearest earl, just because you made a countess of me is no reason to believe that I am now able to perform miracles! A fortnight will not see this house ready for occupancy."

"But you did Beaumanor up so quickly, my dear. What makes this all so different?"

"Pennie, surely with us to help we can do it up much more quickly than that," added Sophie.

"We just must!" protested Sarah. "I do declare that the Temple is not any place fit to live. I am sure I shall never live to see it if I must spend another two weeks there!"

Lady Penelope raised her eyebrows at them, the earl included. "Dear, dear, I never thought it was so serious. Well, I shall certainly have to hurry things along, won't I. My lord, I would explain to you that at Beaumanor, it was merely a matter of moving out the old and rearranging the less old. Here it is a horse of another color entirely. We have got to move out the old, seek out and purchase the new—and much of that will have to be made to our order, don't you see. It all takes time."

"Well, blast the old! Throw it out and get some things that are already available—"

"My dear Lord Dalby, I wouldn't think of it! As you are only an earl, I venture to say it might suit you—other people's tastes—but, as I am a countess, I would not deign to consider such a poor expedient. The Desfords are to have a habitation of which they can be quite proud. You, sir, may decorate your offices and your courtrooms in any manner you see fit, but your home is going to be a place fit for an earl who also happens to be, if you do not mind my saying so, the man I love."

His Lordship grinned. "Don't mind a bit, sweet. Well, go to it and do not spare the horses. I shall abide with patience until you are convinced this place is fit to live in. Actually, if I had had my head on my shoulders in the first place, I should have had all of this setted while we were away on our honeymoon—but that is asking a bit much with you hanging about, my brand-new countess."

"My love, in a moment, we shall both of us embarrass our staff. I pray you will take your leave now while I am still of mind to let you go—or we shall never get on with the important business."

Upon that note, the earl took a fond and de-

cidedly passionate farewell of his countess, leaving
the twins quite breathless—to say nothing of the
flustered countenance of their lady sister as, very
pink of cheek, she gazed fondly after her departing
husband.

As the twins labored along with their sister over
the days that followed, London began to take on a
more appetizing appearance. They were no longer
confined to the closed-in vicinity of the Temple.
Most of their waking hours were now concerned
with the business of the new house on Cavendish
Square where the work of renovation and refur-
bishment went on apace. Sarah and Sophie were
involved in it to a very great extent, relaying the
countess' wishes to the staff and even undertaking
a few minor decisions of their own. But the most
interesting, even exciting, part of it, was accompa-
nying Lady Penelope on her visits to the furniture
makers and drapers to order up the pieces and the
draperies that had been decided upon. Lady Penelope had very definite ideas of what she wanted,
and no one establishment could be found to satisfy
her every wish. As a result, every day saw them going off to another part of town to consult with a
particular tradesman who just might have that
design or that piece of goods that Her Ladyship
had set her heart on.

Oxford Street, Piccadilly, Holborn—every thoroughfare that had a shop of some reputation
sooner or later could expect to be visited by the
Countess of Dalby and her precious sisters. Lady

Penelope, long familiar with the twins' penchant for mischief-making with the shopkeepers of Loughborough and Leicester, warned them in no uncertain terms that she would not stand for any such pranks. They were no longer cute little girls but grown women of sixteen and the Earl of Dalby's in-laws. If they had no respect for her, at least they must have some consideration for him and not make a spectacle of themselves. This last was rather in vain, for the appearance of two such perfect replicas of a beauty could not help to cause comment everywhere they went.

In any case, Her Ladyship's admonitions were not at all necessary. London was not Leicester, and neither Sarah nor Sophie had any inclination to tamper with the Great City—not for the moment at least. They were too much absorbed in the sights and sounds and the great crowds of people that they met with at every turn. There was also the business that they were engaged upon to demand their attention. They were intrigued by all that was necessary to furnish a London townhouse in the first style. It was not at all anything like what it had been at home. Bellflower Cottage was most comfortable, but it was comfort and not fashion that had been called for in its decoration. Most of the houses they had visited were inhabited by families that were devoted to the pursuits of the shire, and they, too, had little to say to fashion. Hunting, horses and farming on acres of land, where any neighbor within a quarter of a mile was considered very close indeed—all led to a style of living that was vastly different from that which they were now in the process of embarking on.

Lady Penelope, herself, except for that one season in London for her coming out, had no experience of the city, but she had learned much of its ways from her perusing of the gazettes and journals and from conversations with the neighbors back home, many of whom came out from the city only for the chase. Then, too, she had her own view of things and was quite determined to see them executed in practice.

When the earl, quite unused to his recently acquired title, had come out to his estate Beaumanor against whose gates the Sandringham's cottage Bellflower nestled, he had asked Penelope to convert his mansion—which his predecessor had used more as a great hunting box than a residence—to a reasonable semblance of a country home. She had done the job quite easily, falling in love with His Lordship in the process. By the time all had been arranged, not without some unasked-for assistance from her sisters, she had had visions how much more fun it would be to do a city place for her love. So here she was, her fondest dream realized and her enthusiasm infecting her sisters.

As far as Sophie and Sarah were concerned, they had begun to look upon the Desford House as their own, especially since Lady Penelope had given them a free hand with a chamber on the second floor to do up as they pleased for their very own.

But there was more. Some few days after they

had plunged into this new undertaking, they had discovered on their return to the Temple that cards had been left. A pair of gentlemen had called: Lord Blessingame and Lord Fallon.

"Oh, heavens, I had clean forgot!" exclaimed Sophie, turning to Sarah. "We were to ask Alan about these two, but the house has quite put it out of my mind."

Sarah sniffed: "It is hardly of any importance. I am just as happy that we were not at home."

"Oh, Sarah, I am sure that they can only have come to offer their apologies. At least, I assume that it is so with Lord Blessingame. Lord Fallon has nothing at all to apologize for. He is a very fine gentleman."

"Then do you be home to him. If Lord Blessingame should deign to come again, I know I shall be out!"

"Now, girls, before we jump to any hasty conclusions, either of you, I shall take up this matter with Alan. You did say that these gentlemen mentioned that they were acquainted with my lord?"

"Their conversation was such as to imply it," responded Sophie.

"Then indeed we must speak to Alan. I am sure he will not care for how you came to meet with them, but we shall just have to risk his displeasure. In any event as we are in no position to entertain, there is not any risk of slighting the gentlemen and we shall have plenty of time to decide if they are proper persons for us to be acquainted with."

"I do not see that that last remark is at all called

for," objected Sophie. "I am sure that Lord Fallon is proper to a fault and I have every intention of remaining at home tomorrow on the chance that he will repeat his call."

"Then you shall stay home by yourself. I have no wish to repeat my meeting with that miserable excuse he calls his friend," said Sarah sharply.

"You may do as you please, sister dear, but I still—"

"Neither of you will stay home now that there is work to be done," declared Lady Penelope. "For one thing it would be most improper of you to receive gentlemen by yourself—"

"Mama can come to stay with me," pointed out Sophie.

"You leave Mama out of this. It is her first trip to London in many, many years, and I shall not allow you to disturb her. Papa tells me that she and Aunt Claudia are having the time of their lives. You are not to interfere, do you hear?"

"But, Pennie, I tell you Lord Fallon is a most respectable gentleman. What, just because you have found yourself a husband, will you deny me my choice?"

"Heavens, Sophie, how you talk! You have but just met the fellow and already you are going to wed him. Now that sounds utter foolishness to me."

"Well, of course I meant nothing of the sort— but how am I to meet anyone while I am here? London cannot be all that different from Leicestershire, and there we were free to entertain Oliver and Percy any time we pleased. Frankly I do not perceive all that difference."

"I could wish Oliver and Percy were about to help entertain you two. After all they are chums from your childhood and their families very well known to us."

"I wish they were here, too. For all their silliness, they are still gentlemen and would never think to insult a lady," said Sarah.

"Now, Sarah, I do wish you would not take it to heart so," reasoned Lady Penelope. "It is obvious to me that Lord Blessingame mistook you—"

"Well, I do declare he has got his nerve! How dare he mistake me for anything so base!"

"Oh, dear, it is not precisely what I meant to imply, my dear. In any case, I assure you there is nothing to pout about. Once the house is finished, I'll warrant you will have more than a mere Lord Blessingame to worry over. Children, I beg you will have but a little patience more. My lord has the greatest plans for you. There is the great to-do over his coming appointment to the King's Bench, then you and I shall make our appearance at Court and beyond that, there will be parties and balls as the season comes on until you will be hard put to choose where you will go for an evening— and do not think that I intend to keep my precious pair of sisters to myself. We shall give our own share of functions, and I should be greatly surprised if you had a poor time at any of them."

"Will you invite my Lord Fallon?" asked Sophie.

"If he comes up to snuff in my Lord Earl's opin-

ion, of course—but I would not set my sights too
quickly, young lady. There will be many young
gentlemen to squire you about, and you, too,
Sarah. Now I pray you will put all this nonsense
out of your minds and help your sister get her new
residence together."

"Very well, Pennie, but you will inquire of Alan
with regard to Lord Blessingame, won't you?"
asked Sarah.

Lady Penelope gave her a look of surprise.
"Why, Sarah, I thought you just got finished telling me that he was a cad and you could not care
less."

"I merely wish to have Alan confirm my bad
opinion of the gentleman is all."

"Oh, I see," agreed Lady Penelope with a mild
little smile and a nod.

Out of the clear blue sky, Sophie mused: "You
know, I sort of miss those two noodles. That is the
one thing London lacks: Oliver and Percy. I wonder what they are doing now—and if they miss
us."

"Have you not written to them in all this time,
either of you?" asked Lady Penelope.

Sarah and Sophie shook their heads, and before
Lady Penelope could express her disapproval of
such a lapse. Sarah rushed on to say: "It would not
have been of the least use. I think neither of them
can read much less write."

"Now that is cruel and most unfair. They were
both of them just finishing their studies, as I re-

call. I am sure some erudition must have rubbed off on them after all this time."

"Well," said Sophie, with a touch of indignation, "there is nothing to say that they could not have written to us. I'll venture to say once we were gone, never a thought of us crossed the feeble excuses they call their minds."

"Well, I am not about to stand about gabbing with you all the afternoon. I must dress for my lord and master and, if you know what is good for you, you will do the same."

"Oh, Alan would never take us to task for any reason. He is too sweet."

"Granted, but he has a perfect horror for wife and she would not hesitate to do so. You may rely upon it, love."

"It just goes to show how mistaken one can be in one's own flesh-and-blood relations," sighed Sarah. "Here I thought that marriage would sweeten your disposition, my lady."

"Oh, you little imp! Be off with you!"

Chapter V

In the great flurry of ordered confusion that attends the arrival of a mailcoach at any English inn, two young gentlemen exited the vehicle and found themselves standing in the midst of a pot of seething humanity known as the yard of the Bull and Mouth Inn, Bull and Mouth Street, London. The taller of the two was looking about him intently, studying the scene, while the shorter, but not by much, gazed in wild-eyed wonderment every which way. A sudden sharp elbow in the ribs by the former delivered to the latter brought about a small explosion.

"I say, Oliver, keep your damn elbows to yourself!"

"Well then, stop staring about you as though you were some yokel fresh from the countryside!

Do you want everyone to take us for a pair of boobies?"

"As it happens that this is the first time we are come to London, I do not see what it matters. We *are* fresh from the country and so are thousands of others."

"Dammit all, it is nothing to be proud of!"

"I ain't proud!"

"Percy, for God's sake, man, use your head! Do you have a wish to be taken for a cabbage head?"

"They can take me for anything they like, but when they take my luggage they'll soon find out how much of my head is made of cabbage. Here you! Where are you off to? That's my baggage you have got!" he shouted and went charging off after a Boots, heading for the portal of the Bull and Mouth, his arms overloaded with bags and parcels.

"See? What did I tell you," shouted Oliver, racing after him.

Great stamping horses and people of all sizes and description were scurrying about, impeding the way, and the two young gentlemen from Leicestershire did not catch up with their luggage until it was well inside the coffee room and deposited at the feet of a great beefy individual in the apron that marked him as the keeper of this great establishment.

Oliver and Percy came up to him all out of breath and looked him up and down, frowning.

"I say, that is our baggage you have there!" charged Oliver.

The innkeeper regarded him with a dull stare

and nodded, saying: "I have got me a fine pair of rooms for a fine pair of gents. First visit to the city?"

Oliver flushed and opened his mouth to deny it, but Percy said, "Aye" and received another poke in the ribs, forcing him back a step.

"My good man, I hardly think that that is any of your business. Yes, we shall take the rooms and have a care with our baggage. Which way to the taproom?"

"Now, how long might you be staying, my fine sirs?"

Oliver looked at Percy and Percy looked at Oliver. There did not appear to be an answer between them.

Said Oliver to the innkeeper: "We shall let you know. Until we have attended to some business in town, we cannot make our plans."

"Why then, my fine sirs, suppose I put you down for two days. Now, if you will be pleased to give me your names, all will be ready upon your return."

They each of them produced their cards and were relieved to see that the innkeeper nodded with approval as he glanced at the Honorable Mr. Percival Deverill's token.

"Be you, by any chance, related to Viscount Deverill, yer lordship?" he inquired.

"His son," answered Percy, matter-of-factly.

"Ah. A very fine gentleman indeed. We have enjoyed his custom in the past, yer lordship. The ol' Bull 'n' Mouth be ever at yer service."

He bowed and then turned his attention to the other would-be patrons who had gathered and were now beginning to clamor for his attention.

Oliver and Percy wandered into the taproom, which was easily found, and stood about a little bewildered.

"Well, are you going to order anything," asked Percy.

"On second thought, I think not. We had better go on about our business."

"I think so, too. How do we proceed?"

"Can I get ye anythink, gents? There be a nice table ready an' waitin'," said a waiter at their elbow.

"Er—no thank you. Percy, let's get out of this. One can hardly think in all this commotion. Egad, doesn't it ever cease?"

They threaded their way out of the taproom, back through the coffee room and into the yard once more. There, the furor had in no way abated.

"Let us find a hackney coach!" shouted Oliver to make himself heard.

"Yes! Where to?" shouted Percy.

"How the ruddy blazes should I know! Let us go for a walk and think on it!"

They thrust their way out of the inn yard, almost getting run over by a departing coach in the process, and proceeded down the street at a brisk pace.

Coming to a confluence of many streets, they stopped and gazed across the teeming intersection in great bafflement.

"Ah, yes," said Oliver. "I do believe I am beginning to get my bearings. Do you see yonder great dome?"

"Who can miss it? 'Tis St. Paul's, I vow," replied Percy, unimpressed.

"Well?"

"Well, what?"

"Why, St. Paul's is quite a noted landmark. One can see some part of it from almost any point in London, I'm told."

"That is hardly a landmark to do us the least bit of good. We already know we are in London," retorted Percy.

"Yes, I dare say you have a point. Well, what do you suggest we do?"

"Are you asking me?"

"Well, of course I am asking you. Must I do all the thinking for us?" snapped Oliver.

"By gad, no! You would only overstrain yourself, my lad. I suggest we go to the Temple. We know that that is where they are."

"Lord and Lady Dalby, but that is not to say that Sophie and Sarah are with them. There is their Aunt Claudia, you know—and furthermore, we cannot be sure that Judge and Mrs. Sandringham are not in separate residence, and the twins would most likely be with their parents, I should think."

"Well, do you know where their Aunt Claudia resides or where the Sandringhams are staying?"

"No. Do you?"

"No, I do not, old chap," said Percy with great

forbearance. "Therefore, I suggest we go to the Temple and seek out Miss Pennie, for we know that she is there with the earl and is bound to be in possession of her sisters' direction."

"I say, Percy, you have got it wrong, you know."

"I am sure I do not."

"Yes, you do. She ain't Miss Pennie any longer. Lady Pennie?" he asked, his face screwed up in thought.

Percy brought his hand up to his chin. "I hardly think so, Oliver. Lady Dalby, I should think."

"Well, yes, to the rest of the world—but she was always Miss Pennie to us, don't you see. Surely it could be Lady Pennie. I do not think she would take exception to it, do you?"

Percy thought about it for a moment and then shook his head. "Oh, I don't know! I say we ask her when we find her. Let us proceed to the Temple."

"Excellent suggestion, old boy," replied Oliver. "Which way is it?"

Out of patience, Percy wheeled on his friend and cried: "I have not been in this ruddy place a blasted second longer than you have, you out-and-out bonehead! How the devil should I know!"

"Well, how in the devil are we to find it?" retorted Oliver.

"We'll hire us a hackney coach and let him find it!" shot back Percy, and turning about, he hailed one while Oliver muttered: "Now, that is what I suggested right off, I'll have you know!"

A well-worn rattler pulled up to them, and the

coachmen hopped down from his box and opened the door for them. "Barnaby Atwell at yer service, gents! Where be you for?"

"Let me handle this," said Oliver, thrusting Percy to one side. "My good man, would you happen to know where the Temple is located?"

Barnaby Atwell drew a long face and pondered the complex inquiry for a moment. " 'Tis a bit of a ride, sirs. London be a great place."

"Well, I am sure we all know that it is, but the point is, how far is the Temple from here."

The coachman had been studying his fares rather intently and he replied, very soberly. "Nigh on ter three mile it be."

"Good lord!" exclaimed Oliver. "I had no idea that London was so great!"

Percy then stepped forward and peered at the medallion on the man's breast. "Ah, seventy-three, is it? I had best make a note of that."

"What the devil for?" demanded the coachman, truculently.

"I dare say you have guessed that we are newcomers to the city. Well now, I have been advised, if ever I have a doubt as to a hackney fare, I should take down the driver's number and report it with all of the details to the commissioners. Would you say I have been properly advised, my good man?"

"Oh, Lord love me!" exclaimed the coachman. "A pair of narks. Ah, sirs, it was just a bit of joke, ye see. I never meant any harm in it. Ye'll not turn me in now, not fer a bit o' fun, would yer?"

"I believe we were inquiring as to the where-abouts of the Temple."

Barnaby Atwell, all agrin, began to rub his hands together. "Ah, ye be a pair o' right uns, right enough! Hop in, gents. The Temple it is and nary a penny will it cost ye. No sir, Barnaby Atwell is a right un, too!"

Oliver began to grin as he made for the carriage but stopped when he heard Percy say: "Whatever the legal fare is to the Temple is what we shall pay, fellow. Just get us there and be quick about it!"

The gentlemen took their seats and the hackney started up.

Oliver groaned. "Percy, you had it all your own way! Why did you ruin it?"

"I didn't ruin anything. The chap has got to make a living, doesn't he? It is just that I resent being taken for a dimwit just because I am not a Londoner."

"Well, I told you how it would be if you insisted upon going about all cow-eyed."

"And I told you it would not make a bit of dif-ference— Oh, I say, will you look at that! We are here already! 'Nigh on ter three mile it be.' Hmph!"

They got out and paid off a very obsequious driver, who was more than a little relieved to see the last of such dangerous fares.

"I suppose that this is Temple Bar and all be-yond is the Temple. You wouldn't happen to know the number of the earl's house, would you?"

Oliver shook his head. He was somewhat subdued.

Said Percy: "Actually, we could have walked here. We shall know better next time—but I am at my wits' end as how to proceed. We can hardly go about knocking up all the inhabitants of the place in our search for the Dalbys."

"It appears to me that an inquiry at any door should elicit the information. If I had an earl for neighbor, I should bloody well know it."

Percy turned an appreciateive grin upon his friend. "I must say, sometimes that noodle of yours manages to come up with a good idea. Not often, but sometimes."

Nose up in the air, Oliver stalked into the great enclosure of the Temple and went up to the first door. Percy waited behind him.

Oliver's point was well made, and they were politely informed that the Dalbys could be found at No. 6 and weren't the two young ladies a pair of darlings.

Greatly encouraged that their long search was at an end, the two gentlemen quickly repaired to No. 6. Oliver raised his hand to the Dalbys' bellpull and Percy pulled it back.

"I think we are rushing things, old chap. Really, we are a sight. Just look at us. We look as though we just got off the stage. Should we not freshen up a bit and make ourselves presentable?"

Oliver brushed Percy's hand off his arm and replied: "You do as you please. I think it is a sign of our devotion that we stood upon no ceremony but came right to their door the moment we arrived in town."

"Well, all right. I dare say I am as anxious as you are to get a sight of them."

Oliver retorted: "Now, are you quite sure that all is in order and I may ring?"

"Quite. Go right ahead, old chap."

He gave a hearty tug, and in a moment they heard someone descending. The door opened and a young maid poked her head out. As she regarded them, her face reflected something less than enthusiasm at their seedy appearance. She did not bother to address them, merely looked an inquiry.

Said Oliver, from a great height: "Pray inform Miss Pennie we are come to call upon her and her sisters."

If anything, the maidservant's look grew more distant. "There are no Miss Pennies in this household, sir! This is the residence of the Earl of Dalby."

"Well, dammit, girl, I am well aware of that! Oh, I beg your pardon! The thing is that we have known Her Ladyship since she was Miss Pennie— er, Miss Penelope? We are neighbors of hers from Leicestershire and have come to town to pay a visit."

The maid regarded him somewhat insolently, looking him up and down. It was quite obvious she was not prepared to entertain his claim.

Percival shouldered him aside and presented his card to the girl. "Here, lass, take my card into your mistress without delay. Truly, Oliver, you do go about things in the most difficult way. I say miss, why do you stand about?"

"Mr. Deverill, I be instructed to inform all who may call upon the family that Her Ladyship is not receiving at this time. Announcements will be sent out at the proper time."

"Oh, that is quite all right. Do but take our cards in to her. We are very close to the family and do not stand upon ceremony with them, don't you see," said Oliver.

Marked disbelief appeared on her countenance as she shook her head. "I tell you, sirs, it is no manner of use. Her Ladyship is out."

"What of the Misses Sandringham?"

"They be out, too."

"Very well. We will be obliged if you will inform the earl that we would like to have a word with him."

"He be out, too, sir."

"Bless my soul!" exclaimed Percy. "I dare say that we shall just have to wait, then, blast!"

" 'Tis no manner of use. You see they are all engaged with the new residence in Cavendish Square. We all of us shall be removed to it in a little bit. Of course, this is no proper place for an earl and his lady, as I am sure you will agree. So I suggest that you come back in a fortnight or go to Cavendish Square. Then, perhaps, Her Ladyship will receive you."

Percy turned to Oliver. "What do you think?"

"Damme, but we shall be doing no good for ourselves hanging about here. I say let us go to Cavendish Square—"

"Oh, but, sirs, you dare not!" protested the maid. "I have just informed you that Her Ladyship is not receiving—"

"Tend to your own business, girl! Come, Percy, I did not come down to London for the purpose of standing about engaged in idle chatter with maid-servants!"

He turned abruptly away and began to stalk off. Percy said to the maid: "I pray you will not mind my friend. He is out of sorts after our travels—but do you give my card to Her Ladyship in any event. Good day."

He came up with Oliver and demanded. "What makes you so cranky, pray?"

"Well, it seems to me that if we go to all this trouble to come to the city and succeed in locating our neighbors, they at least could have the decency to be about when we finally do show ourselves."

"I suppose there is no hope for it. You talk like a fool because you are a fool. So they are not here. What of it? At least we have an idea where they are at. Now, I would take it as a personal favor if you would button up your lip and allow us to get on with it. I am not in the best of humors either. Eleven hours on the stage is no prescription for joy."

"Quite. Now how do we get to Cavendish Square?"

"I still think we ought to go back to the inn and change before we make our call."

"No. We have wasted enough time as it is. I say 'Onward!' "

"Then we had best make inquiry of someone as to where the place is."

"We could go back and ask the direction of their maid," suggested Oliver.

"No, we cannot. Not after your boorish behavior toward her. She'd not give us the time of day now."

After further debate and conference, they reached the smashing conclusion that any passerby who looked a Londoner might do just as well by them. This proved to be the case, but the directions to the Square were rather complex, so that once again they had to put their fate in the hands of a London hackney. They were dropped off at the sidewalk bordering the square and they stood for a bit, looking about them, examining the buildings on the four sides, trying to induce from what they observed which of the edifices might house the objects of their search.

Finally, Percy tapped Oliver on the arm. "There! Over there! That great house, one of four. The middle one, I do believe."

"Why do you think so?"

"I just saw Jepperson at the window. It has to be!"

"I thought he was at Beaumanor. How does he come to be here?"

"How the devil should I know. He is here and so that must be the place. Come along," and Percy started off across the square with Oliver alongside.

Lady Penelope was standing in the great hall, looking disconsolately about her. Jepperson looked at her, waiting for her to speak.

"There was no sign of the carters, Jepperson?"

"Not a sign, Your Ladyship. If Your Ladyship wishes, I can send round to Chippendale's to learn what is causing the delay."

The sound of bare knuckles sounding on the front door broke into their conversation, and the countess remarked: "You have not seen to the bell yet, Jepperson. I wish you would before we have callers. That must be the cart from Chippendale's now, thank goodness. Mercy! But there is so much to attend to!"

Jepperson had gone to the door and the countess was about to leave the hall when she heard him exclaim: "Mr. Deverill and Mr. Grantford! What a blessed surprise! Oh, I am positive Her Ladyship will be grateful for faces from home!"

Lady Penelope, with a smile of welcome on her lips, cried out: "Oliver! Percy! How delightful!" She approached and held out her hands to them as they eached bowed to her in turn.

Declared Oliver: "My dear Lady Penelope, we must apologize for our distressed appearance, but we have come over, fresh from the stage, to pay our respects. Let it attest to our devotion, which will not abide any ceremony that may only cause delay."

Up shot Lady Penelope's eyebrow as she regarded him with a sharp smile. "My, Oliver, how very gallant of you! Well, I shall not stand upon ceremony with old friends either and, as your dress will not suffer, I bid you gentlemen, both, not to stand upon ceremony and give us a helping hand wherever you can. We can use as many Leicestershire hands as we can find for all the work that remains."

"Oh, I say, my lady, that is a bit much. Would you have us—gentlemen—laboring about the house like a bunch of navvies?" asked Oliver, quite horrified.

"Really, my lady, it is just not done. I mean to say," argued Percy, "this sort of thing is the business of the help, I am sure. Actually, my lady, I must admit to a bit of shock to see you standing about amist all this confusion— A countess to act as overseer is—is incredible!"

"My apologies, Mr. Deverill, for subjecting your tender sensibilities to such a revolting shock. In that case, you may be excused and return to call upon us when all of this confusion is gone and I can be a proper hostess to you."

"Oh, I did not say it was shocking, Miss Penelope—my lady, that is! After all, it is only that you are the wife of an earl. I hardly can believe that His Lordship would be pleased to see his countess in this—er, state—"

"You may rest easy on that score, my dear Percy, for His Lordship has already been and gone. As a matter of fact, I suspect His Lordship is quite used to seeing me thus, as I did do Beaumanor

House for him and I was a mere judge's daughter then."

"My point exactly, Lady Penelope. Now you are a countess and that must speak—"

"Oh, Percy, why do you not go off, you and Oliver, and seek out the twins. I imagine they will be delighted you have come—but I advise you not to get too close to them or they will put you to work even as I have tried."

"Sophie and Sarah are toiling about the house?" asked Oliver unhappily.

"Well, you can hardly have any objection, Oliver, as they are still but mere judge's daughters."

"B—but they are sisters of a countess, my lady."

"Now, fancy that! How bad of me to have missed it," replied Lady Penelope, laughing heartily.

Said Oliver to Percy: "I fear all of this labor has discomposed my lady— Oh, I say, what of Sophie and Sarah. We had better to them."

"I say! We had better," and they rushed off into the depths of the house, leaving Lady Penelope gasping. She turned to Jepperson who had turned aside to muffle his laughter: "They have not changed a bit. I dare say we shall have them underfoot for a bit. At least they will give the twins something to think about. Jepperson, find out where they are staying and see to it that they are moved closer in. I dread having them loose in London, far from any guiding light. What could their parents have been thinking to have let them run off to the city by themselves."

"Well, Your Ladyship, they are eighteen years of age or thereabouts, time when many a chap begins to make his way in the world."

"Oh, Jepperson, you are too cruel. Not those two."

"It might make men of them, Your Ladyship, if you will pardon my presumption."

"Oh, I am not worried for them. It is London I tremble for."

"Strange. I was thinking much the same about Miss Sophie and Miss Sarah," he responded with an impish smile.

Lady Penelope laughed. "I had my doubts of them to begin with and I do believe we had something of a narrow escape, but I got them interested in the house and they have been quite the unexceptional young ladies since. I do not think there will be any trouble from that direction. Once the house is ready, they will be too busy with their social duties to have time for mischief—and they are not children any longer."

"Indeed, Your Ladyship, I am sure it is so," said Jepperson.

"That is what you say but not what you think," said Lady Penelope with a laugh. "Ah, now that *must* be the Chippendale people! Well, you know where the things are to go, so I shall leave you. I have a wish to go below and see how it is with the kitchen and Cook."

Chapter VI

◆

Sarah complained: "This room was just not made for a bedchamber, I am thinking. We have pushed and shoved until I am ready to swoon. I refuse to move another stick!"

She dropped into a chair and stared dolefully about the room. "And we have not even begun to decide upon the drapes and the curtains and the spreads. Oh, Sophie, we shall never get it done!"

Sophie drew up a chair beside her and sat down, nodding. "Yes, no matter how we arrange it, nothing seems to come together. I do not understand it. Our room at Bellflower Cottage was never so difficult. I imagine we must have rearranged it dozens of times and all of them quite pleasing."

"The thing of it was we always had Pennie to help! One of us could always stand back and see how it looked and the others could then shift the piece until it was just so. We need help. We cannot do it *all* by ourselves!"

It was just at that unfortunate moment that Oliver's head came peeking into the room.

"Ah, there you are!" he cried and then, turning to Percy, who was now peering into the room beside them, said, "It's them!"

"Well, of course it's them! Do you think I am blind! Good day to you, Miss Sarah. Good day to you, Miss Sophie," he said to each in turn. "Well, by Jove!" He had the silliest grin upon his face. It was of pure elation, and he nodded to each of the girls in turn again. "Miss Sarah. Miss Sophie."

Oliver frowned and looked at the twins, and then he looked at his friend. Once again he turned to the twins, studied them for a bit and then again he turned to Percy. In strangled tones, he whispered: "How in blazes did you do it? Tell me, man!"

Bewildered but gleeful, Percy could only shake his head and repeat his performance. "Miss Sarah. Miss Sophie."

"Oliver, why do you not take Percy downstairs and find him a glass of water," suggested Sophie. "I do believe the poor boy is overcome."

"An excellent idea. Come, Percy! I wish to have a word with you."

"Well, I did not come all the way down to London to have a word with you, old chap. I came to see Sarah—and Sophie and Miss Pennie—Her Ladyship, of course. Now, I must say it is a poor way to welcome a friend from your childhood, Sarah—and why could you not have at least written a word or two? I mean to say, there we were in old Woodhouse and here you were in London and never a word to let us know how you were doing, whom you were meeting with. I mean to say—"

"I do not care a fig what you mean to say, *Mr.* Deverill!" retorted Sarah. "It appears to me you are taking a great deal more presumption than you are entitled to!"

"Oh, I beg your pardon! I never meant to say anything like that at all, did I, Oliver?" he asked, turning to his friend for support.

Oliver turned to Sophie and said: "I beg you will excuse my friend, Sophie. He is terribly confused, I think. All I wish to say is that I am so happy to have found you, my dear—"

"I think you are confused, Oliver. How could you find me if I was never lost? What has gotten into you two? You are positively giddy!"

Percy frowned. "Look you, ladies, we have come a hundred miles to see you because we have not heard from you, and this is a very poor welcome indeed that you show us. If that is all our friendship means to you, I am going right back home."

Sarah came out of her chair with a warm smile. "Well, of course we are happy to see you, you imbecile! But when you go about nodding at us like a chap who has quite lost his wits, it is awfully difficult to be civil much less cordial. Now, pray what was all that business about?"

"Oh, well, it was really nothing at all. It was just that I recognized you."

Oliver hissed: "Don't give it away, you idiot!"

"You recognized me?" exclaimed Sarah. "Whatever do you mean? You have known me since a child. Of course you recognized me, simpleton!"

"Oh, well, I could always tell it was you or Sophie even from afar. It was when you were both close up that I could hardly ever tell which was which."

Oliver groaned. "That's done it!" he muttered.

"What? You, too?" demanded Sophie.

"Oh, but I can tell you apart now, my dears. It has all come around, you see," Percy hurried on to say.

The twins looked at each other, dumbfounded. Then Sophie turned to the two young gentlemen. "Do you mean to stand there and tell us that you have never been able to tell us apart?" she demanded in shocked tones.

Oliver attempted to put a good face upon the matter. "You will admit it speaks well of our cleverness that we were able to disguise it from you all these years."

"Only because we never dreamed there could be two such numbskulls. What do you think, Sarah?"

"I think it is kind of funny."

The apprehensive looks of the gentlemen quickly changed to grins of relief.

Sophie smiled. "Yes, I suppose it is—and they were awfully clever to keep it from us. What a shame we never suspected. Just think of the fun we could have had with them."

"I think that they owe us reparation." She turned to Percy and said: "Well?"

"Oh, by all means, Sarah. By all means. Whatever you say. Right, Oliver?"

"Ladies, we are forever at your service," declared Oliver, making a sweeping bow.

"Excellent! Then you can begin by moving that little settee over to this wall and setting the bed in its place."

"Bed? What bed? I see no bed," replied Oliver, while Percy gazed about all over the room.

"I say, is this your bedchamber?" he asked, his eyes open wide.

"Well, it will be as soon as we have got it arranged—"

Both gentlemen beat a hasty retreat and stood outside in the hall, not daring to look inside.

Sophie and Sarah burst into laughter and came out after them. Drawing them back into the room with some difficulty, Sarah exclaimed: "Really, this it too much. Percy, such modesty is quite beyond understanding. It is just a room at the moment, and we happen to be in need of assistance to get it arranged properly Now stop being so missish, it is quite unbecoming."

Sophie added: "Now, you promised to make reparation to us, and this is what we require. Are you going back on your word to us?"

"Well, the thing is, Sophie," explained Oliver, "it ain't exactly gentlemen's work, you see. I mean to say, Miss Pennie tried the same thing with us and we had to decline—and she is a countess!"

"Ah, so we do not count with you, is that it?"

"It just isn't done, my dear. Why do you not call upon the servants—"

"Very well, Oliver, you are excused," said Sarah. "You may take your leave, but I am sure Percy did not travel all the way to London just to demonstrate how little our friendship means to him, did you, Percy?"

"I should say not. You know very well, Sarah, how devoted I am to you."

"Of course. Now do you start to shift the settee and then we shall help you with the bed."

"All by myself?" he asked weakly.

Sophie stared at Oliver. "Well, sir, are you going or staying? I do not care which, since it is apparent how little store you set by our friendship, not to say anything about your own word upon it."

There was a look of disgust on Oliver's face as he began to take off his coat. "You know, Percy, this is just how it always was back in Woodhouse. One would think that they could have changed a little for the better by this time. Well, take off your coat, man, and stop staring at me like a befuddled loon. If we wish to maintain our welcome here, we shall have to labor like yeomen."

Moaned Percy, following suit: "This is not at all the welcome I pictured. I say, Oliver, will it always be like this?"

"Oh, do come along now! If Pennie has got the kitchen arranged, after we have done here, perhaps we can have some tea," said Sarah, encouragingly.

"You know, ladies, this could never have happened in Woodhouse," Oliver pointed out as he took up a position at one end of the settee and Percy at the other. "Now, all together, old chum. Heave! Oh, blast! Sophie, where the dickens do you want this bloody thing? It weighs a ton!"

Now the light was beginning to fail, and Lady Penelope was satisfied that little more could be accomplished. In any case, she was expecting the earl to come for his ladies at any moment, and it was time for her sisters and herself to get ready for their return to the Temple apartments.

She called a halt to the activities and turned the reins of authority over to Jepperson, to whom, as butler, they rightly belonged. Sophie and Sarah were sent for, even as a few lamps were being lit, and Her Ladyship awaited her sisters in the great hall at the front of the house.

In a little while the twins made their appearance, followed by two rather bedraggled specimens of Leiscestershine gentry who appeared to be in the midst of a vehement post-mortem on the events of the afternoon.

"And I state unequivocally, you loon, you might have crippled me for life with your fumbling. Why that table crashed down within an inch of my toes as I live and breath!"

"Oliver, you exaggerate!" protested Percy. "It was a good six inches, if I have any eyes in my head to see!"

"Then you don't, blast! I swear I shall be

damned first before I ever venture to move furniture about with you to help!"

"And I shall be damned if I ever consent to move furniture about at anytime, and you may put period to that, by heaven!"

"Pray, what is all this?" inquired Her Ladyship.

"Oh, these two clumsy oafs proved such poor hands with our furniture that it is a wonder there is a whole stick left," commented Sophie.

"And that, my friend, is all the thanks we are like to receive, methinks," commented Oliver, sourly.

"I take it you had more luck with the gentlemen than I did," said Lady Penelope. "If that is so, it is truly a very poor way to remark your gratitude, I must say. Surely Sandringham ladies are more gracious than that."

Sophie turned with a little smile to Oliver and Percy. "Of course. You must know how appreciative we are of your help. You never did mind our ragging at you before. It was never meant spitefully, you know."

Oliver beamed and Percy grinned. Exclaimed Percy: "You may rest assured that we did not take it ill. It is just that it has been a hard day for us. We had so little sleep on the stage, don't you know, that this bit of exercise you put us to was rather like the straw that broke the camel's back. A good night's rest and we shall be all strong and fresh for another day of it. Shall we not, Oliver?"

Oliver gave him a mean look and replied: "I would prefer you let me speak for myself."

"Very well, say it for youself then."

"What is the use of it! You have already said it for me!"

"Then what the bazes are you complaining about?"

"Oh, dear God, they are off again!" exclaimed Sarah. "Pennie, this has been going on all afternoon. A stranger might swear that they were deadly enemies when, actually, they are bosom beaus."

"Yes, I know—but then one can expect little boys to get quite cranky when it is so far past their bedtime," contributed Sophie.

"Now that was uncalled for, young lady. Oliver and Percy are guests in our house—even if it is not all that much of a home yet."

Said Percy: "With all due respect, my lady, if what we have suffered through this remarkable afternoon is how you intend to treat your guests, there can be little hope that you'll have them call a second time."

"Hear! Hear!" exclaimed Oliver in approval.

"Oh, dear, then you gentlemen do not intend to call upon us in the future?" asked Her Ladyship, in despairing tones, her lips twitching nevertheless.

"Oh, well, that is not to say that *I* would not be calling—but then I consider myself a very dear friend to the family, don't you see. Of course, I cannot say as much for Oliver, for he has forbidden me to speak for him."

The ladies burst into laughter as Oliver looked daggers at Percy.

At that moment, the door opened and the earl came in. At once the ladies rushed to him, Lady Penelope winding up in his arms, her lips to his in a very warm salute of welcome.

As soon as she recovered herself—His Lordship looked something radiant, too—she drew back a little from him and asked: "Pray how does the appointment progress?"

He dropped his hands from her arms and shook his head, disgustedly. "It does not—and no one can learn why. Obviously, someone else is making an objection, too, and so it is a standstill for the time being.

"I left His Honor with Lord Ellenborough. They are engaged in a discusson that resembles a debate, and I am beginning to suspect that your father knows very well where the shoe is sticking. In any case, whatever he succeeds in learning from the Chief Justice is bound to be of interest. For the time being, there is nothing for me to do. I hardly expect you would me wish to take up my practice again."

"Oh, Alan, I am sure that you will get your judgeship. Leave it to Papa. He will see to it if any one can."

"You know, my dear, it is the title that is making all the difference. I may be out in my thinking, but I am inclined to believe that the Lord Chief Justice, who is but a baron, has little liking for an earl as his subordinate associate."

"Surely His Lordship cannot be so small of mind as that. After all, it is not as though you would take precedence over him in his own courtroom. He is the Lord Chief Justice."

"I dare say and can only hope that you are right— But, I say, isn't it a bit late for those shop fellows to be hanging about? You there, you fellows, be about your business! It is overlate, and if there is anything further needed of you, you may return on the morrow—"

"Oh, no, Alan. These are not shopmen but gentlemen. They are the sons of your neighbors in Leicestershire—"

"Neighbors? But look at them! They are all over with dust, and their clothes look as though they have never known a pressing iron."

The twins were giggling, and Oliver and Percy, very red of face, were regarding them with angry expressions.

Said Sophie gleefully: "I do not blame you for not recognizing them. They certainly do not look at all presentable, but I beg your forbearance, my lord, for they have come to their distressed appearance in your cause. They are the Honorable Mr. Percival Deverill and Mr. Oliver Grantford."

The earl's eyebrow lifted in doubt as he held out his hand to them reluctantly.

"Oh, come now, Alan, you can put a better face upon it than that. Oliver and Percy have been my sisters' playmates for ever so long. Surely you must have observed them hanging about Bellflower Cottage."

"I suppose I must have, but what the devil have you lads been doing to get yourselves so bedraggled? Surely you can make yourselves up to look something more presentable."

Oliver took a step forward and bowed. "Our humble apologies, my lord, for having allowed you to see us in so reprehensible a state, but we have just this morning descended from the Northampton Stage and, except for a bit of a tea, we have been worked to death by your sisters-in-law. I do not exaggerate, my lord, when I say that this is no fit way to entertain gentlemen."

"You worked? What at, may I ask?"

"At pushing your furniture here and there, my lord. Truly, I must protest, my lord."

Holding his lips tightly pressed together to stifle any sound of the mirth that was welling up inside, he turned to Lady Penelope and remarked: "From the looks upon the phizzes of my sisters-in-law, I suspect, as usual, they got their way."

"Indeed, my lord, it is a sad thing," replied Lady Penelope. "If I could have managed it, I would have, but, no, these two gentlemen insisted upon assisting their former playmates in this hard and dusty labor."

"Is that what we did, Oliver?" asked Percy. "Blast you, how do we manage to get into these coils? I am ready to drop with fatigue. I do declare life in Leicestershire was a deal easier than life in London."

The earl laughed and said: "It is but the labor of true knights in a lady's—er, two ladies' causes. You shall have your reward. I bid you join us for dinner."

"Oh, well, that is a little bit of all right!" exclaimed Oliver. "We'll just hop back to the Bull and Mouth and come calling." He nudged Percy. "You and your complaining! You see, it turned out all right after all. Now, come along, old chap. We have a lot of freshening up to do, and it would not do to keep the ladies waiting. Thank you, my lord."

Percy followed with his thanks, and they both departed out the front door.

"Well, aren't they a pair of noodles!" exclaimed the earl. "I think we are in for a bit of entertainment this evening. You say they are neighbors of ours? How could I have missed them."

"They are forever underfoot at Bellflower Cottage and you would have stumbled upon the pair of them if the twins had not been so bemused with snatching an earl for their backward sister— Oh dear, they are back again!"

And they were. They came in at the door and looked about them very uncertainly.

"A spot of difficulty, old chaps?" asked the earl.

"We are quite turned around, my lord, and as there are not any hackney coaches about, I suspect that we shall have the devil's own time finding our way back to the Bull and Mouth. Could we trouble you to tell us the way?"

"Alan, I have a suggestion that will guarantee that we all of us dine on time. I think we ought to take them up in our carriage to the Temple, and after dinner, we can send them to the inn in our carriage."

"I see the wisdom in your advice, my sweet." He looked at the young men and went on: "Are you gentlemen going to be in town for very long?

"Indeed, sir," replied Oliver, looking in the direction of the twins, soulfully.

"As long as it takes, sir," stated Percy, firmly, and his eyes were gazing in the same direction.

The earl also looked at his sisters-in-law for a moment. Then he said: "Well, you cannot continue to make your quarters at the Bull and Mouth. Suppose I send a clerk to you in the morning to assist you to find proper lodgings, something closer to Cavendish Square. Would that suit you?"

"We should be in your debt, my lord," replied Oliver.

"Forever," added Percy.

"What do you mean 'as long as it takes,' Percy?" demanded Sarah. "What are you up to?"

"Why, all I meant to say was— OOOHH!" He gasped as Oliver's elbow knocked into his ribs.

"For once, my friend, I pray you will allow me to do the talking or surely we shall be in a fine pickle," admonished Oliver. He then turned to Sarah and Sophie with an ingratiating smile: "Percy is something confused and sometimes I am quite worried for him. His choice of words leaves something to be desired."

"Oliver, I'll thank you to keep your elbows to yourself and allow me to speak for *my*self. Do you hear?"

"I hear, old chap, but I assure you there is nothing left to be said. I mean to say, one is a fool to let the cat out of the bag at any time."

"Damned if I understand a word you are saying. Now what was I going to say—"

"Gentlemen, we cannot stand about all evening discussing nonsense. I am sure the ladies have a very strong wish to retire to the Temple as do I— for dinner, if you will recall."

"Of course, my lord," said Percy, looking more confused than ever.

Sarah let out a sniff of impatience and took him by the arm. "Come along you! I swear but you are grown worse since Leicestershire. Percy, how do you manage to get yourself into such a maze? . . ." she was asking as she went outside with him.

Oliver had taken Sophie's arm, and she permitted him to escort her after her sister, but her manner was not particularly warm.

"Would you mind telling me what is actually going on with them, my love?" asked His Lordship as Lady Penelope came up to take his arm and nestled close.

As they proceeded out, Lady Penelope remarked: "It has been going on for ages. The boys are sure that they are madly in love with the twins and so are the girls willing dupes in a great deal of mischief. Oh, Alan, I do not know if it was wise to encourage the young men's company. We just might have our hands full before long."

"I hope not. I was sure that we should be vastly entertained—"

Lady Penelope stopped suddenly and put a detaining hand upon his arm. "Oh, that reminds me. I do believe we might have a spot of trouble already started. Do you happen to be acquainted with a Lord Blessingame?"

"Yes, I have been doing a bit of legal work for him— Oh, dash it all! I have clean forgotten to turn that particular business over to a colleague. I suppose he has called about—"

"No, I know nothing about that. What has occurred is that the twins, against my explicit instruction, went out by themselves one day and managed to attract not only Lord Blessingame's attention, but a Lord Fallon's as well."

"I marvel that they agreed to stay pent up for as long as they did. Well, I do not think there is any harm in it. Both gentlemen are known to me and of excellent reputation. To make sure there is no misunderstanding about our pair of darlings, we shall make a point of inviting both gentlemen to our open house. What say you?"

"I am mightily relieved to hear you say so, and as I am mightily famished as well, let us go or the girls may incite their escorts to go off in the carriage by themselves. I am afraid they are overripe for an adventure—and considering what their last was, I tremble for the future."

As they continued out, Lord Dalby inquired: "Their last? What was that?"

"Hadn't you heard? I was sure you had. They collared an earl for their sister."

He laughed and then he said: "Oh that! It was

not so great, considering all the help that they had from the earl."

They squeezed each other's hands in mutual appreciation and went on out to the waiting carriage.

Chapter VII

———◆———

Lady Penelope was proven wrong. In less than a week, the house on Cavendish Square was not only ready, but the residents and contents of the Temple apartment were removed and resettled in their new quarters. Admittedly, all was not accomplished without the turning of a hair. It was a time of confusion and it called for great efforts from the servants, the twins, the countess and, even His Lordship, the earl. But at last it was done with, and the little family group could relax and try to get used to the conditions of living in a fine and grand city habitation.

Lady Penelope had taken up the station of noble lady but recently. Before her marriage, her only claim to distinction was that her father was judge of some distinction in the distant county of Leicester. It was a distinction that she had held for so long, it was commonly thought it was all she would ever gain in this life. She had shared with her mother a good part of the rearing of the two young beauties who were her sisters and who, with their uncanny resemblance to each other, had gained a remarkable reputation for mischief in the shire. As the entire lives of the sisters had been spent in a large country cottage, Bellflower, the transition to this great monster of a house, situated in the midst of teeming London, was bound to be an experience and, in some respects, a trial. They were used to country roads and country people, broad fields and wild forests spread over rolling hills.

As the earl was almost as new to his dignities as his countess to hers, he, too, was in for a period of great readjustment. Before his unexpected elevation, he had been a sergeant-at-law, a barrister of repute but of no great wealth, and quite content to reside, as a bachelor, in the Inns of Court. Townhouses and mansions were familiar to him only as visitor, and great staffs of servants were a completely unknown quantity to him.

As if all of this green inexperience of London high society and its ways was not overwhelming enough, the chief servitor Jepperson an ancient relic of the previous Earl of Dalby, had started his career as a huntsmen and only became a butler upon the insistence of his former master, a rough and ready lord, who had no patience with niceties of fashion and lived permanently at Beaumanor so that he could be close to the famed Leicestershire Hunt. In short, the beautiful manor house of

Beaumanor was in actual fact a great hunting box, and Jepperson's duties partook more of the hunt than the home. Needless to say, he was often at a loss in his dealings with his new subordinates and often was forced to seek counsel from his mistress, who was in no better case than himself. Fortunately for the household, both Lady Penelope and Jepperson were blessed with a good sense of humor, so that the household managed to muddle along in a rackety fashion which the earl appeared to enjoy. At the evening meal, laughter was frequent, for incidents were related that any proper London matron would have died over rather than have admitted.

But the fashionable world, as ever, was impatient. The phenomenon of two commoners suddenly arisen to the uppermost ranks of wealth and station was something to behold and, upon word having gotten about that Lord and Lady Dalby were now in residence at Cavendish Square, there was a great rush to leave cards and invitations, so that Lady Penelope was quite inundated with social obligations while she was still struggling to make of the house a home.

It was fortunate for all that Lady Penelope was as intelligent as she was pretty or the Desford residence would never have had a chance to survive. It was usually the case that ladies who became countesses were ladies to begin with and had been bred to expect marriage to a high noble. As Lady Penelope had not this advantage, she had recourse to her own resources more often than she liked. But that was not the end of her problems.

By the time Lord Dalby had come to wed his Sandringham lady, he had learned extremely well the lesson that his precious sisters-in-law were in dire need of a hand to guide them and quickly seconded his wife's suggestion that she be allowed to bring them out into society as quickly as possible. The unspoken thought was that it would be a relief to get them married off so that each of them could have her own special keeper—husband was the word they used. In short, Lady Penelope had more than her hands filled, and it was to her credit how bravely she bore up under it all.

For it did not wait upon ceremony for trouble to begin. It started the very day after they had moved in. On the dot of eleven o'clock, two gentlemen came calling. And, while Lord Fallon and Lord Blessingame awaited word that the earl would receive them, two other gentlemen appeared to have their cards sent in to Miss Sophie, Miss Sarah and Lady Penelope.

With an insolence born of indignation, Lord Blessingame and Lord Fallon stared at these strangers, interlopers for sure. Both gentlemen had been congratulating themselves that despite the irregular nature of their meeting with the Misses Sandringham, they were bound to have got the inside track of all their friends and did not doubt but that they should be quickly taken into the bosom of the earl and his relations. Since they were sure they knew all who were accounted fashionable, they felt quite put upon that these two strangers should be able to call directly upon the ladies, especially since they were not in the least fashionable in appearance or any other respect to Their Lordships' knowledge.

Whispered Lord Blessingame to Lord Fallon: "Who the devil can they be? They do not strike me as even being of London. That dress! If that is not a coat cut in the style of two years past, may I lose a bundle at Watier's!"

Replied Lord Fallon: "Whoever they may be, I am sure they cannot be of the least consequence."

"Then how do they dare send their cards in to the countess and her sisters while we must proceed first with His Lordship, pray tell me?"

"Poor relations, perhaps?"

"I pray you are right."

"Really, Jack, you ought to be ashamed of yourself. If these are to be our rivals, then I say thanks be. A more unlikely pair of suitors for those little beauties, I cannot imagine. There is not wealth there, there is not station there, there is naught there!"

"Then methinks you are blind, friend. They are junior to us and that may be an advantage and it may not, but do study the larger specimen a bit and repeat there is nothing there. That is a fine arm and a fine leg. I should hate to have to tangle with him."

"What has that to say to anything? I am sure it is not they we have a wish to tangle with."

Jepperson came in and addressed the noblemen:

"His Lordship will receive you, Your Lordships, if you will be pleased to follow me."

As they prepared to follow the butler, Jepperson turned to Oliver and Percy. "Her Ladyship and her sisters await you in the countess' sitting room, gentlemen."

Very much at home, Oliver and Percy, their eyes still on the pair of London swells, walked out of the room and on into the interior of the house.

Lord Blessingame frowned and said: "A moment, my good man. I do not believe I have had the pleasure of an acquaintance with either of the gentlemen who just left. Could you enlighten me as to their identity?" As he asked, he slipped a note out of his pocket and offered it to the butler.

Jepperson ignored the money and replied: "Your Lordship, the two gentlemen who have just departed are the Honorable Mr. Deverill and Mr. Grantford, both of Woodhouse in Leicestershire, childhood companions to Miss Sophie and Miss Sarah."

"Thank you. You may proceed," Lord Blessingame said, coolly.

They followed him out of the room.

"I tell you, Percy, it is far better that we inquire of my Lord Dalby and do it quickly before we have to make an appearance before strangers," said Oliver as the pair of them came into the sitting room.

Just within the threshold they came to a stop as Percy replied: "It is not as if His Lordship was our parent, chum. We cannot be bothering him about such matters."

"Oliver Grantford, that is no way to come into the presence of Her Ladyship," exclaimed Sophie, shortly.

Both gentlemen immediately came to an awareness of their discourtesy and, both of them stammering a confusion of apologies, hastened to make a proper salute to the ladies.

"All right, gentlemen. Before you break into tears, you are forgiven," said Lady Penelope. "But I do not know what has come over the pair of you. You were always perfect little gentlemen back in Woodhouse. Since we first laid eyes upon you here in London you have never left off bickering between you. Now I want you to begin to mind your manners or I shall send word to your fathers to come and fetch you back to Leicestershire. I am not about to be embarrassed by companions of my sisters acting like bubbleheads before any ladies and gentlemen of fashion who may be present. It not only reflects upon you, yourselves, but on the families who reared you and upon us, who love you."

"My lady, it is unutterable kindness that you forgive us our lapse," said Oliver, bowing deeply.

Lady Penelope laughed and the twins giggled. Said Sarah: "Well, just don't stand there like a pair of gossoons. Do sit down."

Lady Penelope, trying hard to keep a straight face, admonished her sister: "For goodness sake, Sarah, I have just finished wigging the boys for their lack of manners and now *you* have to embarrass me. Is that any way to speak to gentlemen?"

"But they are Oliver and Percy, Pennie," she protested. "What is so special about them?"

"They are gentlemen, my pet, and you had better get used to the idea. This is not Woodhouse. Here, in London, such treatment is insulting and very like to be misunderstood. Would you have everyone believe that you have contempt for our friends?"

Sarah sighed and shook her head. "Oliver and Percy, I beg your pardon. Please be seated."

"Thank you, Miss Sarah," they chorused and took their seats.

Silence enveloped the room as the girls stared at the boys and the boys stared at the walls and the ceilings.

"Children. I never meant to gag you," said Lady Penelope. "I assure you it is perfectly proper to engage in conversation. In fact, it is essential that you do so or what is the point of your call?"

"Why, to be sure that we were your very first callers in your new house," said Percy.

"Well, that's silly!" said Sophie. "You have already been here more times than I can count."

"But it wasn't official because Lady Penelope was not receiving yet," pointed out Percy.

"Well, I do not see that it makes all that much difference."

"Nevertheless, Sophie, it is a very nice gesture," interposed Lady Penelope, "and I do appreciate it. Thank you, Percy. Thank you , Oliver."

Percy nudged Oliver and said: "There! I told you it was the thing to do. You'll think twice before you call me bubblehead again."

Lady Penelope smiled and the twins laughed. Then the silence threatened to engulf them again.

Lady Penelope started a subject: "Pray tell us what you were discussing as you came in. What would you ask of Lord Dalby?"

"Oh that. Why, when we arrived, there were two gentlemen in the hall waiting on His Lordship and they were got up in the latest fashion, I am sure," said Oliver. "If we are to make any appearance at all, we shall have to make the acquaintance of a crack tailor, I should think. These duds will never do for us to go about in while we are here."

"Two gentlemen, you say? asked Lady Penelope. "Did you happen to get their names?"

"Well, no. They were there when we arrived and they did not appear to wish to be spoken to."

Lady Penelope reached for the bellrope and gave it a tug.

"What sort of gentlemen were they?" asked Sophie. "Were they tall?"

"Yes," said Percy.

"No," said Oliver.

The ladies looked from one to other and broke into laughter. Oliver glared at Percy and Percy glared at Oliver.

Just then Jepperson came in.

"Your Ladyship, I was on my way to you. His Lordship sends his compliments and desires to know if you wish to make the acquaintance of some gentlemen with whom he is closeted: A Lord Fallon and a Lord Blessingame."

"Oh, yes!" shrieked Sophie.

Percy regarded her in surprise, but Oliver's face was panic-stricken.

"Sophie! The message was addressed to me. Now do you entertain your visitors while I go to my lord. I shall not be long."

Her Ladyship arose and followed Jepperson out.

Oliver, with a look of the deepest concern on his face, got out of his chair and stood defiantly before Sophie, demanding: "What is between you and these—these fellows!"

"They are not fellows, they are lords!" she snapped back at him.

"I don't give a tinker's dam what they are! I demand to know what is between you!"

"And pray to whom do you think you are speaking in such a horrid manner?"

"I am speaking to you, my dear Sophie, and to no one else!"

"Are you so sure that I am Sophie?"

For a moment a troubled look came into his countenance, and he glanced over to see that Percy was engaged in conversation with Sarah. Now quite assured, he turned to Sophie and nodded. "Yes, I am quite sure!"

"Only after you saw that Percy was speaking with Sarah! Do not deny it!"

Lamely, he replied: "What difference does it make? It is *you* to whom I wish to speak."

"Oliver Grantford, you are a deceiver and I want nothing more to do with you."

"But, Sophie, why?" he pleaded. "We have been friends for ever so long. What has London done to you?"

"Not a thing I assure you," she said, patting at her hair. "Nor do I see that because we are neighbors in Woodhouse it gives you the right to accuse me of anything that comes to your mind."

"Oh, devil take it, I am not *accusing* you of anything. I am making a perfectly civil request of you. What do you and these lords have to do with each other?"

"It is Lord Fallon she is enamored of," declared Sarah.

Oliver stepped back as though he had been slapped, and Sophie turned to her sister, saying: "I'll thank you, Miss Sandringham, to mind your own business."

"Really, Sophie, you are making a cake of yourself. You are treating Oliver quite badly I must say, and you do not even know anything at all about Lord Fallon."

"Well, I am sure that Lord Fallon would not be so dense as to mistake me for my sister after all these years," she retorted.

"Well, I did not say that he is the brightest chap, but he means well."

"Really, Sarah, just because Lord Blessingame did not see fit to get along with you is no reason for you to tell me anything about Lord Fallon— and I certainly am not about to make a cake of myself, dear sister. True, we know very little of the gentlemen, but that is not to say we must forever remain uninformed. If Alan sees no objection to receiving them in his house, I dare say that is sufficient warrant for their respectability."

Said Percy: "I do not see what all this fuss is about. Oliver, why do you not apologize to Sophie so that we can all have a comfortable coze."

Oliver stared at him in outrage. He tried to make a retort but was too dumbfounded to say a word.

Said Sophie: "All of this is a bore. I am going to my room."

"And what shall I say to Lord Fallon if we are asked to meet with the gentlemen?" inquired Sarah.

Sophie made a face and sat down. "Well, I could wish that Oliver did not nag at me so. One would think I had been promised to him."

"Well, I always thought it was understood," said Oliver, trying manfully for a softer tone.

"I was never informed of any such thing, sir," retorted Sophie indignantly.

"Oh, Sophie, you know it was always like that. I mean to say, we were always together back home, all four of us."

"That has nothing to say to it."

Percy frowned and looked at Oliver. "You know, Oliver, I never did think you had the right of it."

"A fine friend you are. What, are you on her side or mine?"

Percy reached up a hand to scratch his head. Finally he shook his head doubtfully. "Oliver, that just does not make any sense at all. If you are going to fight about it with Sophie, I do not see how you can win a thing."

Oliver was going to make a bitter remark to his friend when he paused, looked a bit blank at first and then, as comprehension came to him, his face relaxed and he grinned foolishly. "By damn, you are right, Percy!" Then he looked imploringly to Sophie and asked: "I say, Sophie, my chum is right. It is not something I can fight about. What can I say to you?"

Sophie merely shrugged her shoulders.

Said Sarah: "I do not see what this conversation can accomplish, Oliver. I bid you let Sophie be. She has acquired a taste for London gentlemen it seems, and there is not anything you can say that is going to improve the situation for you."

"Oliver, I do not mean to be contrary but, truly, you have taken overmuch for granted," said Sophie in softer tones than heretofore. "I shall always think of you as a friend—a brother almost—"

Oliver let out a groan.

"Oh, Oliver, why must you make such a fuss!" she ended.

"Bah!" said Oliver. "I wish I never came to London! I am returning home."

He strode to the door and turned melodramatically. Curtly, he asking: "Coming, Percy?"

"Well, of course not. I am damned glad I came to London!"

"In that case, farewell, friend!"

He tore open the door and dashed out.

"Oh dear," said Sarah, looking at her sister with concern.

Percy came over and patted her hand. "There is naught to worry about, my dear. He has not the price of a ticket without me."

The door opened and in walked a crestfallen Oliver.

He could hardly look Percy in the face as he said: "Er—old chum, you could let me have the price of a ticket home?"

Even Sophie had to laugh.

When Lady Penelope came into her husband's office, the three gentlemen arose and Lord Dalby made the introductions.

Lord Blessingame declared: "Countess, it is an honor and an undiluted pleasure to make your acquaintance. I have just been congratulating His Lordship on his recent accession and now I see that further congratulations are in order. Ah, but then I should not have been surprised, for I have had the pleasure of meeting with your sisters. I have a feeling in my bones that before the season is out, the Sandringham name will be on everyone's lips."

In his turn Lord Fallon said: "Indeed, my lady, the Sandringham name has already achieved an illustrious ring to it thanks to His Honor, Judge Sandringham. Now that his beautiful daughters have condescended to bless our city with their presence, the name must bear added luster."

Lady Penelope shot a glance at her husband whose lips were twitching.

"Thank you, my lords. I am flattered to hear you say so, and so, I am sure, will my sisters be when I inform them of your compliments."

The faces of both gentlemen fell.

"Oh, I say!" exclaimed Lord Fallon in his disappointment. "I had hoped that surely we might have had a chance to pay our respects to the ladies before we left."

"Another time, my lord. They are currently occupied. In any case we shall be having a housewarming shortly which I hope you will honor us by attending."

"You may be sure of it—and I thank you for your kind invitation."

"Indeed, my lady," added Lord Blessingame, "I shall not draw breath until that day arrives."

"Oh dear, my lord, I do hope that you can wear blue then. It will go admirably with your complexion," said the countess lightly.

Lord Dalby and Lord Fallon laughed at once. Lord Blessingame was not so quick nor did he seem to get as much enjoyment.

The gentlemen then took their leave and Jepperson came to see them out.

After they had gone, Lady Penelope turned to her grinning husband and laughed.

"I do not know but I think I prefer our Leicestershire Noodles to those London la-di-das, Alan."

"My darling, you shall have to get used to it.

You will be hearing a great deal more of it before you are much older."

"Oh dear! I fear to think what the twins will make of it. They have never been exposed to such flowery speaking before. We are a deal plainer in our tongue out Leicestershire way."

"It will certainly be amusing to observe."

Lady Penelope frowned and said, with a smile: "How comes it that you, a denizen of London and a barrister of note, never addressed me in such high-flown superlatives?"

"For the simple reason, my sweet, that you would have thrown a milk bucket at me, I am sure, if I had."

"Indeed, love, you know me well."

Chapter VIII

Outside the Desford residence, Lord Fallon and Lord Blessingame stood about for a bit undecided.

"It is a bit too early to do anything," said Lord Fallon. "Shall we look in at the club?"

"Why don't you go ahead, Frank. I needs must think a bit and shall stroll about while I do it."

Lord Fallon laughed. "You do not fool me for an instant, old chap. The countess was a surprise, wasn't she?"

Lord Blessingame grinned and cocked an eye at his friend. "It strains one's credulity, doesn't it? She is more a countess than Desford is an earl, Some fellows have all the luck, blast!"

"Oh, I say, Jack, surely you do not begrudge him his good fortune?"

"Well, of course I do not. It is just that I should very much like to have a piece of it myself."

"Yes, I know what you mean. But, as I recall, there is a piece or two of that same luck laying about, chips off the old block in a manner of speaking—except where Her Ladyship may be deemed handsome, the sisters must be acclaimed beauties."

"Well, now, that brings up those two lumps we remarked waiting to see the ladies—Deverill and Grantford. I worry about them."

"I say! We cannot stand about in front of their house all day. Let us move along, Jack. We can talk while we walk."

"An excellent idea."

As they began to stroll along the square toward Oxford Street, Lord Blessingame remarked: "It is a bloody shame! Nobody knew about those sisters-in-law. We should have had the entire field to ourselves for the start at least."

"Oh, for heaven's sake, man, what is there to complain about? Surely you do not think two such poor specimens can compare the least favorably with ourselves, do you?"

"Oddly enough, under this set of circumstances, I would not be prepared to wager heavily against them. These are Leicestershire ladies and *they* are, for all their ratty attire, Leicestershire gentlemen who have known Miss Sarah and Miss Sophie for ages. That is bound to count heavily in their favor. After all, what do we know of rural beauties? They are bound to require a different sort of handling than ladies with a deal of town bronzing, don't you see."

"No, I do not see. *I* had no great difficulty with Miss Sophie."

"Oh, stop your crowing! You were just lucky. I am sure you had the very same estimate of the ladies as I did, right off."

"But I kept all of my doubts to myself—which is always the best policy with any strange females."

"Very well, I admit I acted without thinking—but how am I to get into her good graces now? I had hoped that this call upon Desford would have given me an opportunity to speak with her. I could have made an abject apology. I imagine that even in Leicestershire apologies are made and accepted."

"Somehow, old chap, I do not think you came off too well with Her Ladyship. The setdown she gave you spoke volumes in that regard. Something of a wit there."

Lord Blessingame gave his friend an unhappy look. "Do you think she is going to be a dragon?"

"It stands to reason that she is not about to allow her sisters to be thrown to the wolves."

"I do not think I care for your metaphor, friend."

"Oh, you know very well what I mean. We have got to watch how we step with her."

"I am beginning to wonder if the game be worth it. Sounds filled with mantraps."

"Indeed, I should not mind being caught in one—Sophie by name to be precise."

"Yes, you make a good point—but those two bumpkins! There was an 'Honorable' amongst 'em. Deverill."

"Could be the son of an earl, perhaps a viscount—look him up in *Debrett's*. But, at the same time, we had better not overlook Grantford."

"Why should we not? He has no no rank."

"The trouble with you, Blessingame, is you do not survey the field before you advance. Now I took the trouble to look up Judge Sandringham. I am sure that Her Ladyship was not unhappy to hear me praise her father."

"Yes, I thought that was rather sly of you."

"Call it what you will, but it did nothing to hurt my chances, I am sure. You could use a bit of slyness yourself, my friend."

"I find I am forced to agree. Very well, we can find out about Deverill easily enough, but Grantford is a commoner. Where do we find anything about him?"

"At the club. Sir Roscoe is a huntsman of old, and Leicestershire is noted for the sport. I venture to predict that the old gossip will know everything there is to know about the Leicestershire families."

"I say! Sounds a most excellent idea. Come along, old man. To the club it is!"

It was not very long after Lord Blessingame and Lord Fallon had departed the scene that Oliver and Percy came out of the house to stand in the very same spot that they had but recently vacated. Their conversation was somewhat more animated than that of the previous pair of gentlemen.

"So you call yourself my friend and yet will not

advance me the price of my fare!" exclaimed Oliver, heatedly.

"No. Why ought I? I should be left quite alone in the city."

"Very well, then come home with me."

"No. Why should I? I am getting on famously with Sarah, and that is precisely why I came to London in the first place."

"Well, I am not getting along with Sophie, famously or otherwise. I am not getting on with her at all. I am sure she has eyes for those London swells. I warned you, Percy, how it would be, the girls all by themselves in London."

"Nonsense, I warned you! In any case, it was you who needed the warning, not I. Sarah has eyes only for me.

"The devil she has! It is just that she has not met a dandy to take her eye yet—but she shall! Mark my words! Then where will you be?"

"Well, I am blamed if I shall be in Leicestershire while all of that is going on. I expect to be Johnny-on-the-spot and see to it it does not happen."

"And pray just what do you think you can do to prevent it, my friend? Do you think you can compare favorably with these London lords?"

"By heaven, I shall show them a Leicestershire lord who can make them sit up and take notice!" exclaimed Percy, fiercely.

"You!" hooted Oliver.

"Look you, Oliver, there is no one to say that I

cannot style myself Lord Deverill. I am the son of a viscount you know."

"Bah! You are an 'Honorable,' never a 'Lord,' and you know it."

"Well, the chances are most excellent that I shall *be* a lord someday!"

"But you are not one now and that is to the point. Oh, what the dickens are we arguing about! It is not going to be a title or anything else that decides, it is going to be what the girls want and, if they can have a London gentleman to squire them about, I do not see them looking in our direction."

"Well, blast you!" exploded Percy. "You knew it might be that way when you started out. Why did you come if it was only to be defeated."

"Well, I did not think that Sophie would have turned fickle so quickly. By the way, how did you manage to tell them apart? You could at least have given me a hint."

"Well, actually, I really do not know, old chap. I just seemed to have known it was Sarah as soon as I entered the room."

Oliver sighed. "I should have known better than to have asked. You are never a help to me. Well, since I am bound to remain in London until you make up your mind to leave it, what am I supposed to do?"

Seriously, Percy answered: "I am sure I could not wish for a better brother-in-law than you, Oliver; therefore, I am bound to assist you in this predicament. We ought to think about it."

"Fat lot of help that will be. While we are thinking about it, there is one of these lords stealing away my intended."

"Actually, Sophie was never your intended, old chap. I am sure she never thought so."

"If that is what you truly believe, my dear Percy, as much can be said for Sarah. Perhaps we ought to think about *that*!"

A worried look spread over Percy's countenance. "I say, perhaps we ought to speak to Judge Sandringham right off. It is what we would have done if he had been at home in Woodhouse. I do declare the situation is become quite trying."

"I do not see what difference that would make. Sophie is barely civil to me."

"Well, we have got to do something!"

"All right, let's do it. I do not see how it can hurt anything."

As Oliver's and Percy's footsteps died away in the corridor, Sarah looked at Sophie and remarked: "You were very unfriendly to Oliver and he coming all the way from Leicestershire just to see you."

Sophie sniffed. "See me, indeed! With what, may I ask, since his eyes cannot distinguish me from my sister?"

Sarah raised a hand to her eyebrow uncertainly. "Oh, surely they could not have been serious. They must have been joking. It is inconceivable that they cannot tell us apart after all these years. How come, if it is true, we never tumbled to it?"

"Perhaps we are not so clever as we thought."

"Or they are a deal more clever than we could have believed," suggested Sarah.

The twins looked at each other in some surprise for a moment, each one given to a serious consideration of this most unlikely possibility.

"I think we shall have to look into the matter," said Sarah. "It would be perfectly awful if it turned out that somehow Oliver and Percy had been making us their dupes all the while."

Sophie nodded. "Yes, I quite agree—but how shall we go about it?"

"It is quite the simplest thing. All we have to do is to trade partners every now and again without their getting wise to it and we can tell, from how they deal with us, whether or not they know it is you or it is me. You realize, of course that your new gentleman friend will have to be involved— and, I think, we would be wise to bring in Lord Blessingame as well."

"Well, I think not!" replied Sophie, indignantly. "You may bring in Blessingame if you wish, but I see no reason why we have got to bring in my Lord Fallon."

"Well, I mean to say, we have got to have some-one else into it, one for you and one for me just in case the boys have got some sort of signal worked out. I'd not put it past them."

"Oh pooh! Those two chuckleheads? Never, on my life, would they be so clever."

"Percy is not a chucklehead! He is just a bit—er, slow."

Said Sophie, in a bit of a pet: "I don't know if I

care to bother. After all we are grown ladies now and quite beyond that sort of thing."

"It is hardly a question of that at all! How would you like to wind up married to a man who thought you were your sister, pray?"

"Oh, I could expect that if it were Oliver I had married, but I can assure you Lord Fallon would never be so deceived."

"Then what is there to object to? In any case you have got to do it for me. I mean to say that if Percy does not truly know how to distinguish you from me, I had better know it now then later."

Sophie raised an eyebrow and regarded her sister as she asked: "Is that how it is between you two? I never thought that you saw anything in him."

"I am not saying I do, it is just that there is always the chance, especially if he has been coming it over me all of the time. I say we have got to be sure—and that goes for Lord Fallon as well. Sophie, you have only seen the gentleman but that one time. As your loving sister, it is my duty to insist that you make sure."

"Oh, it sounds a child's game!"

"It is a most serious matter, Sophie."

"The thing is I am not marrying Lord Fallon. He is but a friend—"

"Well, you might wed Oliver, and how would you feel if he declared himself to me thinking it was you—or Lord Fallon for that matter?"

Sophie grinned. "Perhaps you are right. In any case, if *any* of them has been pulling the wool over our eyes, it will go to teach them all a lesson. Very well, let's do it!"

Away from the main promenades, off on a foot-path in Hyde Park, two gentlemen were thoughtfully strolling along, neither speaking to the other. Deeply engrossed in their separate thinking, their ambling along was obviously quite aimless. They were two typical London gentlemen but out of the top drawer of society. The one of them was frowning and the other seemed to be at peace with himself.

Lord Fallon, happening to glance at Lord Blessingame and seeing his expression, inquired: "What's troubling you, old chap? A penny for your thoughts."

"Too cheap by far, friend. I'll wager you'd offer a pound and more to know—and you'd not be grinning either after I told you."

"Oh, come now, Jack! How can anything be so bad on as lovely day as this. Ah, I know what it is! You are still in a pet over the treatment your beautiful Sandringham dished out to you. Admit it now!"

"Well, I am not at all pleased with it, but that is but a small part of the matter. Give me but a few moments with the lady and it will all be made right."

"I dare say!" drawled Lord Fallon, sarcastically. "You always did fancy yourself as quite the ladies' man."

"Devil take it! My manner with a lady is unexceptional, and in polite society an apology, properly delivered, must ever be accepted or we would have very little polite society left, I tell you."

"Granted, but that does not make your further advances to the lady in any degree more welcome."

"I say, old chap, be a good fellow, won't you, and allow *me* to worry about that?"

"Quite—but then what is there left to worry about?"

"Surely it is as plain as the nose on your face! They are twins! Have you ever thought that there will come a time when you have got to distinguish between them?"

"I can't say I have, for I do not consider it as any problem at all."

"Then you had better peer into that poor excuse for a mind and reconsider it."

"Well, I still do not see the difficulty. Whichever of the ladies I address, it is for certain that she will respond to Miss Sandringham. For the time being, it is enough and will serve quite adequately."

"The devil it will! You appear to forget those two lumps from the shire who undoubtedly have been on a first-name basis with them for ages. If it should prove that there are others amongst our set, too, who have known them long enough to tell them apart, we must certainly be the outsiders and will have more than our fair share of work cut out for us. Think, man! While we are muddling about, never sure of which of them we are addressing, other chaps will be getting quickly to the point with them, something we do not dare to do until we know that it is Miss Sophie or that it is Miss Sarah we are speaking to. What if I should make my apology to Miss Sophie? Calling her Miss Sandringham would be not a bit of help in the situation."

Now Lord Fallon's brow was creased in thought, and he came to a stop. Lord Blessingame faced him and said: "A bit of a sticking place that, isn't it?"

Lord Fallon looked up at his comrade and said, wryly: "I could wish you had not brought it up, blast you! What in blazes are we to do? There is no time! The Desfords' affair is tomorrow night!"

"I told you so! Now you see how much my penny's worth of thought amounts to."

"That is hardly worthy of comment," snapped Lord Fallon. "We have got a desperate situation on our hands. I love you like a brother, Jack, but this is the first time I find your absence more desirable than your presence. I say, would you consider not going to the Desfords' tomorrow night?"

"Most certainly not, nor do I see how that would help any."

"Well, if you were not about, I could be my sweet and charming self to both the Misses Sandringham and never have to worry whether it was Miss Sophie or Miss Sarah I was addressing. If you call yourself friend to me, you would not come."

"And if you call yourself friend to me, you would not ask it!"

"Well, I did not truly expect you would see it my way—but it does put us deep in a pickle and no time to get us out of it."

They both of them were silent for a few minutes while they contemplated this queer turn, each of them giving vent to a sigh of frustration and a shake of the head.

Then Lord Blessingame gave a start. "I say, I have got an idea!" he exclaimed.

He was so excited he grabbed his friend by the lapel, and so interested was Lord Fallon to hear him that he gave but the merest wince at the cruel grip crushing the life out of the delicate material.

"Frank, we have got to get to Deverill and Grantford!" he cried. "They have got the secret, don't you see. They will know how we are to tell the ladies apart!"

"If they would be so kind! What the devil makes you think that they would put themselves out for us when they are obviously on the same track. I cannot imagine any man knowing the twins for as long as they have and not dangling after them."

"Aye, there is that," agreed Lord Blessingame, discouraged. "But you will admit it is our only hope. We have got to look the chaps up and engage them in a discussion, somehow get the ladies into it. You leave it to me."

"Yes, leave it to you. Just as you did with Miss Sarah. I think you had best leave the talking to me, my friend—"

"Look you, Frank, the circumstances were such that—"

"They were precisely the same for me and I wound up having a delightful chat; whereas you—"

"Let us not go into it, I pray. Well, whoever

tries, it is not going to be all that easy, I tell you. I think it will call for stronger measures than clacking our jaws at the them."

"Hmmm, what do you have in mind?"

"I say we invite them over to the club and feed them all the brandy that is necessary to loosen their tongues. In that way, I'll wager, we'll get us a description of the ladies the way they see them and we shall have our clue."

"Sounds a very promising way to go with them."

Lord Blessingame and Lord Fallon turned about and marched smartly back down the path.

There was a sharp rapping on the door, and Oliver, lying stretched out on a couch in the sitting room, disturbed the newspapers over his face by reaching out a hand to Percy, who was sitting on the window seat, looking out.

"Be a good chap, Percy, and see who it is."

Percy turned from the window to stare with great disapproval at his chum and roommate. "Really, Oliver, I do not see what you wanted to come to the city for if all you are going to do is to drowse the days away."

The newspaper cascaded to the floor as Oliver sat up. "Now how the devil was I to know that Sophie was going to be cool to me? I'd have gone right back home like a shot out of a gun if my dearest friend had not shut his pockets to me."

There was a further rapping on the door, and Percy went to answer it, replying: "A better friend than you think. Surely you cannot believe it is all over for you with Sophie. I mean to say— Yes, what in bloody blazes do you want?" he exclaimed to the Boots as he swung open the door.

The lad held up a pair of cards in his grubby hand and said: "They be two gem'ums ter see yer, Mr. Dev'rill."

"Yes, well—just a moment," Percy said, taking up the thoroughly besmudged pieces of pasteboard and studying them. "I say, Oliver, what do you think?" he exclaimed as he turned from the door. "It's those two chaps we saw at the Desfords'. Do you recall them?"

He handed the cards to Oliver, who was now standing up in his shirtsleeves, his hair all tousled from his hands rubbing at his head.

"Fallon and Blessingame? Now what brings them to us? Have you any idea?" he asked as he studied the two cards.

"Not a smidgin. Fancy two such swells going out of their way to call upon us."

"Well, we best have them up. We shall never find out what this is all about else."

"An excellent idea— You, Boots, show the gentlemen up."

As the Boots sped away, Percy turned to stare at the room about him. "You know, old chap, this place is becoming something of a sty. At least comb your hair and put on a coat."

Oliver nodded and did as he was bid. As he carefully patted his forelock into place before the mirror, there came a knocking on the door. Percy went to answer.

Lord Fallon and Lord Blessingame came into the room in a rather grand manner, looked about them for a bit, repressed slight shudders and then devoted themselves to Oliver and Percy in a flurry of introductions and handshakes.

Said Lord Fallon: "Saw you chaps at the Desfords' and thought it would be an excellent idea to make your acquaintance. You are new in town, are you not?"

With breathless anticipation, Percy and Oliver assured him that that was the case.

He went on: "Well then, as any friend of the Desfords' must be friends to us, we had hoped to find you in a mood to see the town, take you about, don't you know. Introduce you at our club—all that sort of thing—that is, if you are not otherwise occupied."

Having been assured that they were completely at liberty and delighted at the opportunity to go about the city in such distinguished company, Lord Fallon gave a knowing glance to Lord Blessingame and replied that he and his friend were at their service.

Short moments later, they had trooped out of the apartment, down the stairs and into Lord Blessingame's carriage, neither Percy nor Oliver quite sure why they were there but almost giddy with excitement and grateful for the opportunity.

White's subscription room was filled with its usual population of members gathered into small groups about the tables provided for cards, engaged in games of chance or merely chatting as were the two noble gentlemen and their guests.

At the moment Lord Blessingame was casting impatient glances at Lord Fallon, who was looking back at him with a rather helpless expression.

Oliver was giving an authoritative lecture on some of the chases he had been on back at Leicestershire and had a devoted audience of precisely one, namely Percy. On the table was an empty bottle of brandy and one that was down a quarter.

Abruptly Lord Blessingame arose, bringing Oliver's recitation to a halt.

"Your pardon, gentlemen, but I have something I wish to discuss with my lord. We will be back with you in a moment. Why do you not pour yourselves another to pass the time."

Lord Fallon arose and joined Lord Blessingame in a nearby alcove.

"Now, I say this business has gone far enough! What is it with those two? Have they no bottom? Our purpose was to get *them* primed. I tell you another drop and it is I who shall be all squiffy. How are you standing up to it?"

Lord Fallon glanced back at the table and groaned. "Just look at them. They are still at it. Good heavens! I think they breathe the stuff! What manner of men do they rear in Leicestershire."

"Well, we can hope that their wits are not in any great shape. We had better get on with it—drunk or sober—or we shall be in no condition to hear what they may have to say."

"Agreed. Let us return."

They went back to the table and sat down.

"I say, are you chaps enjoying yourselves?" asked Lord Fallon.

"Indeed, my lord. This is a bit of all right. We have nothing like this in Loughborough," replied Oliver with a happy grin.

"Ah, Loughborough. Is that where you reside?"

"No, my lord. It is the largest town in the area. Actually Percy and I live in Woodhouse. 'Tis a bit of a village on the border of Beaumanor, the estate of the Earl of Dalby."

"Ah, yes, Woodhouse. Now that's got a familiar ring to it. I say, Blessingame, where have we heard that name before?"

Lord Blessingame looked surprised. "The Sandringhams have a place there. Don't you recall?"

"Thank you, my friend. Indeed it does come back to me, now that you mention it. Why then, our friends here must be neighbors of Her Ladyship as well as His Lordship. It explains the term of affection Her Ladyship used when referring to our friends here. You gentlemen must be very close to the family, I take it."

"Very close indeed," boasted Percy. "Why we knew the countess when she was Miss Pennie— Of course, we do not address her so these days, you will understand."

"Of course. I hear tell that there are more daughters in the Sandringham family. I dare say you must be as well acquainted with them?"

Percy frowned and Oliver's eyes opened wide. It was the latter who made reply.

"Naturally, my lord."

"The countess is quite a handsome female. How is it with her sisters?"

Percy opened his mouth to make an objection only to feel the elbow of Oliver jabbing him into silence.

Said Oliver: "I beg your pardon, my lords, but it becomes necessary for my friend and me to engage in a bit of conversation. By your leave, my lords."

He hauled Percy up out of his chair and drew him over to the very same alcove.

"Well, what did I tell you? They are up to no good. I think we had better start putting our heads together."

"Oliver, I am sure I do not follow you. They have only asked after Sophie and Sarah. I see no harm in that."

"Oh, don't you see, man, there is something suspicious in it. After all, we have had it from the twins themselves that they are acquainted with these two. So how comes it that they must inquire of *us* as to Sophie and Sarah?"

"Now that you mention it, it *is* devilishly odd. What do you think they have got up their sleeves?"

"I'm dashed if I know! But I say that we should go cautiously with them."

Percy nodded enthusiastically. "Indeed we ought—but how shall we go cautiously?"

Replied Oliver, uncertainly: "Just go cautiously

and watch what you say. Now, let us return to the table as if we do not suspect a thing."

In the meantime, back at the table, Lord Blessingame snorted disdainfully: "Well, Fallon. you have gone and got their wind up, it seems."

"Now how is that possible? I merely inquired after the countess' sisters. What is so terrible in that?"

"I haven't the vaguest idea, but just look at those two. Suspicion is written all over their faces."

"Hmmm, yes. Well, we are in to the business. I see no point in backing out of it. We might get something new from anything they say— Ah, there they come!"

Oliver and Percy nodded at their new acquaintances and resumed their seats.

Lord Fallon thought it wise to try a new approach and said: "Gentlemen, let me be frank with you." Throwing out his hands to emphasize his complete openness, he declared: "It is known to us that you are both of you on the best of terms with the Misses Sandringham—"

Oliver looked disgruntled and gave a little snort. Lord Fallon and Lord Blessingame exchanged glances, the former going on to say: "—and we come to you to beg a favor."

"What the devil!" exclaimed Lord Blessingame.

"Hush, Jack! We are all of us gentlemen of honor and must come to the point without the least subterfuge."

"Ah—yes, of course. None whatsoever."

"Exactly," said Lord Fallon. "Now, my friends,

it is but a small favor we require of you. It will cost you nothing and can only work to your advantage to grant it."

"What is it you ask?" said Oliver, still regarding Lord Fallon with suspicion.

"As you have known Miss Sarah and Miss Sophie all of your lives, it stands to reason that you cannot have the least difficulty in telling them apart. Now, of course, you realize that it is not the same for us. It will take us a bit of time before we are well enough acquainted with the ladies to be able to do as much. All we ask is that you tell us of the qualities that distinguish the ladies in your eyes."

"Now why on earth should we wish to do that?" demanded Oliver.

"Because it cannot hurt you in the least and we should be your friends forever."

Percy declared: "You ask too much, my lord. Heaven knows the difficulties I have had upon that very score with the ladies. I am not about to assist another chap to the portal I have struggled so hard to attain."

Oliver regarded Percy with surprised approval. "Hear, hear," he murmured.

"For heaven's sake, Deverill, you mistake our purpose completely," protested Lord Fallon. "You suspect us of intending to pay suit to the ladies, and it is not the case at all. How could it be? We have but the slightest acquaintance with the family and even less than that with the ladies themselves. I tell you what it is. It is simply that

Lord Blessingame, here, has a matter to address to them and it would be most embarrassing if he were to put the particular point to the wrong lady. It could be the cause of the gravest misunderstanding, don't you see—an embarrassment, not only to himself but to the Desfords and the Sandringhams as well."

"Really, Fallon, you could have put it another way, I am sure," remarked Lord Blessingame, greatly annoyed.

Lord Fallon rejoined, in sweet tones: "I promised there would be no subterfuge and there is none, even at the cost of your discomfort, my friend. We cannot have Deverill and Grantford mistake, for an instant, our perfect honesty upon any point."

Lord Blessingame turned a sour look upon him but did not comment further.

Percy opened his mouth to speak.

"Cautious is the word, chum," warned Oliver.

Percy looked at him in surprise and said: "I do not see what caution is called for. What they ask of us is impossible. I know *I* can hardly tell the ladies apart much less tell anyone else how to go about it. And, as for you, Oliver—"

"Oh, shut your mouth!" snapped Oliver. "Gentlemen, my friend speaks the truth. We are not able to assist anyone when we have so much difficulty ourselves."

"Now, that is not being friendly in the least, Grantford!" shot back Lord Blessingame.

"Leave this to me, I pray, Jack," said Lord Fallon.

"Look you, gentlemen, what you have just stated is an insult to the intelligence of a flea. You cannot expect us to swallow so great a whopper. I mean to say when one gets to know a pair of twins, one is bound to finally recognize the little differences that exist between them. Here you have been their acquaintances for lo, these many years. It begs all credibility that you should have least trouble on that score now."

"Well, the fact is precisely that, incredible or no!" said Oliver.

"Look you, sir, I am not a dimwit and can never believe that either of you is so dense as never to have been able to distinguish between the friends of your childhood!"

"Blast you, my lord, it never was of the least importance before!" retorted Oliver, heatedly. "It was never our wits that were at fault, it was simply not a necessary thing, my lords! I mean to say, what difference did it make when we were young whether it was Sophie or Sarah that we addressed or which was which? They were the same, don't you see, nor do I recall that it made any difference to them for the longest time. It was only when we got to thinking of the consequences after our marriage— Well, that is surely of no concern to you, my lords. I have said enough."

"Not by far!" retorted Lord Fallon. "We are not to be taken in by any such Banbury tale as that, sirs! I warn you if that is your story and you intend to stick to it, I shall enjoy spreading it all over town. You chaps will be the laughingstocks of the city and will have a devil of a time of it. It will be overlate to change your tune then."

"Aye, and what will the ladies have to say to it, do you think?" asked Lord Blessingame. "How happy will they be to learn that such close friends as you have been to them have the greatest difficulty telling them apart?"

"Good show, old man!" exclaimed Lord Fallon as a look of guilt spread over Oliver's and Percy's faces.

But, as Their Lordships saw only defeat there, they pursued their course, never realizing how thoroughly they had demoralized their opponents.

This time it was Percy who nudged Oliver. "Come on. We have got to have another little chat, friend."

"Excuse us, gentlemen, if you please," said Oliver, getting shakily out of his chair to follow a worried-looking Percy back to the alcove.

"Neat, what?" said Lord Fallon, grinning triumphantly at Lord Blessingame.

"Can you imagine those noodles trying to pull such a cock-and-bull story over us?" replied Lord Blessingame with a satisfied laugh.

"Well, now the fat's in the fire for sure!" exclaimed Oliver.

"Oh, but isn't it though! Why, if Sarah should ever get wind of this, she'll never let me hear the end of it through all of our married life together."

"You idiot!" hissed Oliver. "What makes you

think she will *want* to marry you after this gets out?"

"Hang it, you're right! I say, this is very bad, old chap. We can't let them say any such thing. I think we shall have to challenge them to a duel."

"No, no, never think it! It would only make matters worse. The reason for the affair would get about and it would all be for nothing. Sarah still would not have you."

"But, I say, Oliver, we cannot just let them say what they please, especially as we have gone to so much trouble to keep it hidden from the girls."

"We shall just have to tell them something. It will be enough to quiet them."

"Oliver, I absolutely refuse to do any such thing. I shall never reveal my secret— In any case, I don't think I could even if I wanted to."

"What the devil do you mean by that? Of course, we shan't tell them the right of it, but you do have got to tell *me*!"

"I tell you I cannot. I do not know how I do it myself. After all, it is quite new to me. I mean to say, we came upon the girls this once and there it was. I knew that one was Sarah and therefore the other had to be Sophie."

"Well, I knew *that* much!"

"No, no. I knew Sarah at once is what I am saying!"

"Then if you had not seen them together, you still would not know for sure which was which?"

"How can I say until I *have* seen them apart?"

Oliver groaned. "Oh, what a pretty pickle this is!"

"Well, I am not saying I wouldn't know Sarah apart from Sophie, I am just saying perhaps, you see."

"Well, how do you do it? You can tell me that much at least."

"Why, I do not rightly know. It is just Sarah when it is Sarah. There is something different about Sarah."

"But that is precisely what I am trying to find out from you. What is the difference?"

Percy stared blankly at Oliver and shook his head. "It is a feeling. How does one explain a feeling?"

"You could not explain anything, you shuttle-head! Well, we shall have to go into it another time. I should have asked you before this. Why didn't you remind me? Never mind! We have got to tell my lords something since they will not see the truth of the matter. Do you have any ideas?"

"Tell them anything, just so it will shut them up."

"But they will soon find out that we have bubbled them," pointed out Oliver.

"By then it will be too late for them. They will already have made fools of themselves with the girls, don't you see, and nothing they could say in their defense would be believed, I am sure."

Oliver pursed his lips thoughtfully for a moment. Then he nodded and said: "Yes, I believe you have it right. Now then, what shall we tell them?"

"Why, it really does not matter. Ah. I have it! We shall tell them that Sarah's left eyebrow is the slightest bit higher than her right."

"Is it really!" exclaimed Oliver. "I never noticed."

"No, you numbskull!" retorted Percy with impatience. "I do not know it is that way at all. It is purely a ruse to make them think they have got the secret!"

Oliver raised a hand to his brow and nodded comprehendingly. "Of course. I do not know what has come over me, Percy. I am absolutely petrified over this business and cannot think clearly."

"Oh, pull yourself together, man! The worst of this mess is far from over. Remember, you are in no better case than they are with the girls."

"That, my friend, is precisely what has me aground! Let us get back to Their Lordships and give them this very special bit of news."

Chapter IX

———— ◆ ————

On the very day that the Desfords' opening their house to the fashionable world was to commence the various snarls in the Department of Red Tape were either unraveled or cut through, and it filtered down through channels and into the higher levels of a gossiping society that Alan Earl Dalby could now be addressed as His Honor and would shortly take his seat in the Court of King's Bench. It is hardly worth mentioning that any of those very high-in-the-nose worthies who might have been debating the merits of attending the Desfords' housewarming came immediately to the conclusion that it was not an affair to be missed. The fact that both the earl and the countess were so new to their rank and privileges could count for nothing against the importance that this professional elevation conferred upon His Honor Earl Dalby.

So it was that the house in Cavendish Square was baptized in a stream of the finest specimens of English Fashion and Nobility. The affair actually was a rout. There was no dancing or anything beyond a few refreshments supplied for entertainment nor were there anything like the number of chairs required for the huge crowd of guests. No one expected more. It was enough to have been invited and be allowed to exchange a few words of congratulations with the new celebrity and his handsome consort. At least that was the purpose the guests had when they arrived, but their aims were brought quickly to great confusion when they beheld the very remarkable phenomenon of a pair of young beauties so very similar in every detail of lineament, dress and gesture that they were forced to rub their eyes to be sure that they were not seeing double. In short, Lord Dalby's appointment was completely outshadowed by the appearance of his sisters-in-law, Miss Sophie and Miss Sarah, who stood with him and Lady Penelope to greet the incoming guests. They were quite the sensation of the evening, and no one could doubt but that they would be the sensation of the season.

As for the twins themselves, they were not in the least abashed. They were quite used to the excitement their appearance had always given rise to wherever they went. That London was proving itself no different rather added to their self-confidence than diminished it. And that was not good, for self-confidence was the one quality the twins never lacked. It was as though they were a person multiplied by two, their forwardness and audacity coming in for more emphasis than their other traits.

As they stood with their noble brother-in-law and sister receiving all sorts of high flown compliments upon their beauty and charm, Sophie's eyes were frequently busy searching the throng, and only until Lord Blessingame and Lord Fallon came forward to pay their duty to the host and his ladies was she suddenly quite at ease and something more warm in her manner.

On the other hand, Sarah's manner underwent an icy transformation, so that there never could be any difficulty in distinguishing between the two young beauties if one had but the key to the reason for the difference in their demeanors.

Their Lordships had not the least difficulty, therefore, not that it would have made any difference. Both ladies could be addressed as Miss Sandringham.

There was a courteous exchange of conversation, and since Lord Blessingame addressed some of his remarks directly to Sarah, she had no choice but to respond.

To the earl he then said: "With Your Lordship's permission, I beg leave to pay my addresses to Miss Sarah."

"So quickly, man? You have but just met her."

"Oh, well, I mean to say—well, that is, my lord, I do *not* mean to say that I intend to begin my suit with the lady. There has arisen a misunderstanding between us which has been the cause of great unhappiness to me. I would rectify the situation."

The earl smiled and shrugged. "Certainly I have no objection. What say you, Sarah?"

"If His Lordship has a wish to call, it must be my pleasure to receive him," she replied in distant tones.

It was as much as Lord Blessingame could have hoped, and he stepped back into the crowd with a slight bow.

Lord Fallon soon followed him, and both gentlemen departed the Desford residence for another affair with satisfied smiles upon their faces.

"I wonder what was said," commented Oliver to Percy as they stood a small distance from the earl and his party. "Sophie looked too pleased by far to satisfy me."

"I say! You are getting better at it, old chap. It *was* Sophie that was all smiles."

"Well, it had to be Sophie, because Sarah is still on good terms with you and she was not smiling, don't you see."

"Yes, there was that. But, blast, Their Lordships had no trouble distinguishing betwixt 'em. Do you think the bit about Sarah's eyebrow actually did the trick for them after all?"

"Oh, how should I know? Come, let us go up to them and pay our respects—and find out what has been doing."

The house on Cavendish Square was dark. All of its lights were out with the exception of one, high up on the third floor—the bedchamber of Miss Sophie and Miss Sarah. They of all the Desford household had still not retired. Oh, they were quite exhausted from the ordeal of the rout and mighty well pleased with the sensation that they had caused; but, from the expressions upon their faces, they were less than completely satisfied with the evening. Although in fact they were dropping from exhaustion, they were not about to drop off to sleep until they had aired to each other the particulars of their disappointment.

Said Sarah: "It did not work. It could not even begin to work. There were just too many people about."

"Well, really, Sarah, when you presented such a long face to Lord Blessingame, a child could have guessed which of us was which. In any case, 'Miss Sandringham' is an address which will never give anything away. It was very wise of you to have given me a signal not to keep up the pretense as it never could have worked. I suggest that we give it up."

"No, it is too important a matter. Look, Sophie, it is still quite simple—but we must go at it a little more slowly, more deliberately. Actually, I have been thinking that the way we are about to start was quite unfair to Oliver and Percy. You see, they must needs address us as 'Sophie' and 'Sarah,' whereas Lord Blessingame and Lord Fallon can make do with 'Miss Sandringham' for either of us.

You will admit that that is a distinct advantage of Their Lordships?"

"Ye-es," agreed Sophie, "that is true enough. How are we to get around it?"

"Simple. We have got to cultivate Their Lordships so that very shortly they will be on closer terms with us and must begin to call us by our Christian names. Only then can we prove what we are out to prove."

"Well, actually, Sarah, what precisely is it that we are out to prove?"

"Oh, you goose! We are trying to determine exactly how clever Oliver and Percy are."

"Well, I do not in the least object to it. I think Lord Fallon is quite a handsome gentleman and charming. I should like it very much indeed if we were to get on closer terms."

"Well, that is not the point at all."

"I understand, but I do not see how *that* can hurt a bit."

"Yes, well, then you must remember that Their Lordships are in this, too. It would not be at all fair of you to give Lord Fallon any hint once we have switched."

"Oh, Sarah, a little help in that direction is not going to set the plan astray. I am sure I do not wish to see His Lordship embarrassed."

"Oh, well, in that case, I shall see to it that Percy is not in danger of being embarrassed either."

"But then what would be the point of all this? I do not care a fig whether Oliver knows me or not. It is you who have to test Percy."

"All right," agreed Sarah. "But, for the same reason you have got to test Lord Fallon, don't you see. What's fair for Percy is fair for His Lordship."

"Oh, very well," retorted Sophie, grumpily.

"I mean to say if you give clues to Lord Fallon and I give clues to Percy, they each will give clues to Lord Blessingame and Oliver and then what would be the point of it all?"

"I said 'all right,' Sarah. Now for heaven's sake I pray you will stop up your mouth and let us get to sleep. I am positively exhausted and I would not be surprised if Lord Fallon should come calling in the morning."

"Good night, sweet sister."

"Good night."

But Fate was being more capricious than usual those days, and no one of the various sets of plotters appeared to be satisfied with the progress that they were making.

Said Lord Fallon to Lord Blessingame as they strolled along Oxford in the direction of Cavendish Square one morning: "They came it over on us, that pair of Leicestershire loons! I say, we ought to be bloody well ashamed of ourselves to have allowed them to take us in so! Her right eyebrow is higher than her left! Hah!" he snorted.

"I believe it was quite the other way about, old chap," returned Lord Blessingame, mildly.

"What's the difference! It was a bunch of bloody nonsense to begin with. The ladies' eyebrows are perfectly even and beautiful to boot! Blast those country Captain Sharps!"

"I say, Frank, you are making a cake of yourself. All right, so they took us in. Put it out of your mind and apply yourself to the problem at hand. We shall be there shortly and you have still to determine a scheme by which you will be able to tell Miss Sophie from Miss Sarah."

"Yes, and it is getting more and more imperative that I succeed. Miss Sophie has warmed up to me in a marvelous fashion and I have no doubt that I shall not be able to address the lady as Miss Sandringham much longer. Actually, any other lady and I should have been on a first-name basis with her ages ago. Oh, why did she have to be twins!"

"The game is too much for me. There is no question in my mind but that they are a pair of beauties whose like is rarely seen, but I am not about to plunge myself into the very self-same sea of embarrassment in which you are wallowing. I learn my lesson quickly, old man. Let a female be a bit less a beauty just so long as I know I am speaking to her and not her sister."

Lord Fallon gave a glance of impatience at his friend. "Bah, it is just a case of sour grapes with you, my friend. You missed your chance with Miss Sarah right at the start and have never been able to make it up with the lady—although I could swear she was quite cordial to you when we paid our call the day before yesterday."

"Aye, that she was," agreed Lord Blessingame with a nod. "For the first time I had the pleasure of exchanging some words with Miss Sarah without it felt like a cold draft blowing down my back. There is no gainsaying it but they are charming creatures when they are of a mind to be."

Lord Fallon nodded enthusiastic agreement. "Indeed, but you are right, Jack. Why with the pair of them so graciously sweet, one did not dare take his eyes off whomever he was speaking with, for fear that he would not know her again. Oh, dear God!" he suddenly exclaimed, clapping a hand to his forehead.

"I say, old thing, will you kindly take yourself in hand. People are beginning to stare!" complained Lord Blessingame. "Why do you cry out?"

"Jack, I just had the most dreadful thought! Do you realize that if Miss Sarah continues to be as sweet with you as Miss Sophie is with me we are lost! We shall not have a clue, I tell you!"

Lord Blessingame frowned. "By George, you are right! Oh, say, lad, I am getting out of this right away. I leave to you all of the fun and frivolities. It has suddenly become much, too much, for me," he said as he came to a stop.

Lord Fallon turned and looked at him, his eyes a bit wild. "You are not going to desert me now in my time of greatest need, are you, dear friend?"

"Indeed I am! I suggest you do, too, dear friend, for you are headed for a bruising fall."

"Jack, I beg of you to come with me at least this once. Good heavens, man, can't you picture how it will be for me, having to deal with the pair of ladies at one and the same time? You must come and

help to keep them apart so that I may devote myself to Miss Sophie."

"Well, all right, Frank—but just this once, you
hear. You are not to rely upon me in the future. I
have had my bellyful of the Misses Sandringhams,
sour grapes or not."

That afternoon, in their lodgings, the two young
bachelors from Leicestershire were voicing com-
plaints of slightly different nature.

Oliver was saying: "You only have yourself to
blame, you know. It was your idea to tell them
that business about Sarah's eyebrow. Now see
what has happened. They are able to distinguish
between the twins so well that you are in a way to
lose your interest with Sarah. She is being unduly
affectionate to Lord Blessingame, I should say."

"But I tell you there is nothing to it! I have
looked myself, just to be sure. After all, I manufac-
tured the bit out of whole cloth, so I ought to
know if anyone does. I looked, I tell you, and there
is not a thing wrong with Sarah's eyebrow."

"Ah, but are you sure it was Sarah's eyebrow
you were looking at? You know, chum, you are but
new at the game and it could very well have been
Sophie's."

Percy stared at Oliver and scratched his head.
Finally he shook his head and cried: "Oh, devil
take you! You are always making difficult situa-
tions impossible! I tell you I was sure. After all, I
do know *my* lady, even if there are some of us who
do not!"

"No call to get so nasty, chum," snapped Oliver. "If anything, it only makes matters worse and you would see that if you had but half a brain!"

"There you go again! Making matters worse! What is it with you, Oliver? I pray you will keep your disappointment at Sophie's manner to you to yourself, for that it is that is making you so surly."

"Well, you had better get a little surly yourself, you fool. If Sarah is making up to Blessingame and he to her, it appears to me that he must have some secret way of telling them apart of his own—or it is Sarah who is taking the lead in the business."

"Why, she would never!" exclaimed Percy with heat.

"Never, you say? Is Sophie so different? See how *she* is behaving!"

"Yes, but I am me and you are you and there's the difference!"

"Oh, good lord, Percy, you are not making a grain of sense!

"Truly, Oliver, I begin to regret not having advanced you your fare home. I have half a mind to do so on the instant."

"Aye, half a mind!"

"Oh, do shut up!"

The two friends glared at each other for a while and then, pointedly ignoring each other, resumed their toilets and finished dressing. Still not exchanging one word, they left the house and began to stroll toward Cavendish Square to make their daily call at the Desfords'.

As they approached the portal, a massive mantel supported by two multi-colored stone balustrades framing the door, two gentlemen, heavily engaged in conversation, stepped out into the street.

Upon seeing Oliver and Percy, Lord Fallon ceased abruptly his earnest discourse to Lord Blessingame and turned to them with a nod. It was not a friendly nod, but it was more than a mere acknowledgment of their presence.

"Well, gentlemen, we meet again, do we. I cannot say it is a pleasure for me, because it is not—but I have a word or two to say to you."

They had come together now, and Lord Fallon poked his first finger into Percy's chest in a most insolent fashion as he went on to say: "So you thought to take us in, did you? Hah! The left eyebrow so very slightly higher—indeed! Well, I am pleased to tell you that your little ruse did not work. In fact, I am beginning to think it will not be long when I shall be able to tell the ladies apart without the least hesitation. You may take your tricks back with you to Leicestershire. They'll give you no advantage here in London."

Said Oliver, angrily: "I would suggest that my lord is taking his fences far too soon. You may think you know Miss Sophie from Miss Sarah, but you never can be so sure. I, who have known them since their pigtail days, ought to know. Don't you agree, Percy?"

"Indeed I do—"

"Then you are indeed witless. There are differences between them. It is just a matter of sorting it all out, and *that* does not require a lifetime. You are still trying to come it over on me. Well, you are wasting your breath. I'll wager that in less than a fortnight, I shall know to which of the two ladies I am speaking just as readily as you. Good day to you, sirs! Come, Jack, I see no advantage to us to continue with this conversation."

Lord Blessingame and Lord Fallon linked arms with each other and, noses on high, marched away across the square.

As they left, Oliver idly watched them as a thoughtful frown creased his brow.

"I say," he said softly. "Did you hear the fellow?"

"Well, I was right alongside. Of course I heard him and I thought he was being particularly nasty. But what the devil does he mean 'it is just a matter of sorting it out'?"

"Precisely. It is precisely what I am thinking about. Now, look you, Percy, before we go inside, you have got to put your poor excuse of a mind to work and explain to me, down to the smallest particular, what goes on in your thinking when you look at Sarah and know that she is Sarah."

Percy regarded Oliver with a blank stare and said: "There is nothing to explain. I just know it is Sarah and I am right."

"Now, how do you expect that that will be of the least help to me, you bloody fool?!" ranted Oliver.

Percy shook his head. "Oliver, it becomes more and more difficult to get along with you with every passing minute. I must keep reminding myself constantly that you are my chum from boyhood. Now, don't you think I would tell you if I could?"

Oliver beat a hasty retreat. "Heartfelt apologies, old chum. I should not have flown off at you like that. Regrets and all that sort of thing, don't you know. The thing is that I am beside myself. I mean to say, I have always taken it for granted that Sophie was mine forever and that we must wed after a matter of time. Suddenly it is no longer so! Now just stop to think how you would feel if you saw Sarah taking the greatest pleasure in the company of another man. Stop and think on it for a bit, Percy."

"I do not have to. I have already seen it. She has been making eyes at that Blessingame fellow in a way she has yet to look at me." His voice grew pained as he spoke. There was a teary quality in his tone as he went on: "Oliver, old friend, what is happening? Are we about to lose the loves of our lives forever? I am sure I could never bear it."

"Easy on, old man, easy on. I mean to say, we have not lost them yet. It is early days before there is any talk of settlements and marriage vows, don't you know. Courage, Percy, all is not lost yet— And that is precisely why, my friend, you must put your mind to it—even if you have to strain it to the utmost—to discover how you can tell Sarah from Sophie."

Percy shrugged. "Since I have not the vaguest idea where to begin, we should be at the business all day—and I have a wish to see my Sarah immediately. I had no liking for the smug expression on

Blessingame's phiz. I say, that fellow is downright dangerous to have loitering about one's lady."

"Well, if I had to pick between them, I'd much prefer him to Fallon where Sophie is concerned. Now there is as cool a fish as ever I could hope to see!"

"Well, then we had best go on in immediately and see what damage has been done to our prospects."

"No, not a step until you tell me something. I do not like this helpless feeling. I mean to say, I do not dare to go in to the ladies unless you are with me and I must keep my mouth shut until you have addressed Sarah so I shall know Sophie. My God, what were I to do if ever you had to leave town and I had to go in to them all by myself?!" he exclaimed, his features screwed up with worry.

Percy regarded his friend with a pained expression. "Oliver, all I can say is it is a feeling. I look at the girls and there *is* something different between them. Sarah is just—just more Sarah-ish, if you can follow me."

"Sarah is more Sarah-ish?" asked Oliver in a weak voice, a look of puzzlement growing on his features.

"Yes. I do not know how else to express it."

Oliver put up a hand as though to stop his friend and bent his head in thought for a moment. Finally he looked up and said: "By George, Percy, I do think you have got it! Much as I hate to admit it, Blessingame's remarks were indeed a revelation to me. Now, with what you are saying, it is all beginning to make sense. You see that, don't you?"

"I do not see anything at all."

" 'Sorting it out, man'! That is the whole business in a nutshell. I just never took the trouble to sort the girls out is all. I mean to say I never truly thought about it, there had never been a need to. It seems to me I have been a bit stupid about this."

Percy shrugged. "That, my lad, is hardly news."

"Oh, don't you go all high-and-mighty over me, you chucklehead, just because you came to it first. You just stumbled on to it, whereas I shall *think* my way to the discovery of how they differ."

"If you can! I do not see that it matters how you come to it so long as you come to it."

"In that you are being shortsighted. If you do not understand the difference—that is, if you have not gotten them truly sorted out in your mind—you can never be totally sure that you will not mistake Sophie for Sarah at some time in the future when it can be most important. I must hand it to Blessingame. He does have the right of it. I am not too proud to follow what he said and I shall start to study most diligently our dear ladies."

"Now, just a moment, Oliver. You study Sophie to your heart's content but leave Sarah strictly alone. *She* is my business and you know it!"

"Oh, you confounded ass! I have got to study both to see the differences and get them sorted out. How can I do that if I restrict myself to Sophie?"

"Well, I do not like it!"

"Think, man! It is turn-and-turn-about with us. *You* would be well advised to study Sophie as well as Sarah to make sure you truly are aware of what you are about. I shall have no objections, because I understand the necessity of it. For goodness sake, Percy, you do not have to be jealous of me. I love Sarah like a sister, it is Sophie I would wed."

Percy regarded Oliver glumly, trying to think of a further objection.

Oliver went on: "Look you, there is Blessingame playing the very same game by his own admission. And there is nothing you can do about it. I suggest that you worry about the attention he is paying to Sarah and leave me to work out my way with Sophie the best way I can. I may have Fallon to contend with, but you have got Blessingame— And, if we do not get cracking on it, I'll wager we shall be having every eligible chap in London to contend with, blast!"

Chapter X

For all of their lives up to the present, Sophie and Sarah had been twins in every conceivable way. Not only did they look exactly alike and attire themselves to preserve that impression, but their every gesture, their every expression was never a clue to give them away. In their early days, Mrs. Sandringham had found it most convenient to dress them alike. It was so much easier to construct their little garments from the same pattern rather than to do all the cutting and extra work required in preparing different gowns for each of them. As they were adorable dressed as reflections of each other, it went on that way until the twins themselves discovered what a marvelous thing it was for making mischief. From that point on, they themselves consciously worked to keep the small differences between them concealed as much as possible.

The members of their immediate family, of course, had no trouble in distinguishing between them, and they, themselves, had naturally assumed that Oliver and Percy, their childhood chums, knew them. They never stopped to consider that the occasional mistakes the boys made were anything more than what occurred at home when actually the boys referred to each of them with the first name that came to mind. In short the odds that the right name would be applied to the right twin at any particular time were even steven.

Nevertheless, Oliver and Percy, for all their preoccupation with their own growing up, unconsciously sensed the difference that did exist between Sophie and Sarah, and gradually, each boy began to favor his own particular twin; Sophie was Oliver's particular interest and Sarah Percy's, as far as that sort of thing goes with young gentlemen before their thoughts turn to love and romance with great intensity. It was a matter of sheer panic to the young men when they came to realize that suddenly it was a matter of the greatest importance to know, and for sure, which twin was which at every moment of their existence. Since they never had been required to put their minds to any great tasks before this calamitous realization came to them, it was not surprising that they were making something of a hash of the business, working themselves into a perfect lather of confusion.

Sarah's plot to determine the nature of their deceit would surely have unmasked them at once, if it could have been put directly into practice, but, as the girls discovered, it was not an easy thing to do. Their delay in executing the plan allowed Oliver and Percy a period of grace of which, of course, they were not aware.

The major obstacle to hinder Sarah and Sophie in their attempt to switch identities was the presence of the countess. Lady Penelope was long used to her sisters' preoccupation with mischief and would have found them out the very instant they had tried to fool any one. The twins knew their sister well and had been under her management back at Bellflower Cottage as much as they had been under their mother's. Now, Lady Penelope was no less sensitive to their comings, goings and doings (as guests in their sister's house) than she had been before her marriage, and they knew they must tread carefully.

The frustration had little if any effect upon Sophie, but, upon Sarah, it was quite noticeable. For the first time in their lives, the sisters were drifting apart in their thinking. Although they themselves were not aware of it consciously, this new and, to them, strange state of affairs started to add to the tension of the time. Sophie grew more and more reluctant to go through with the plan, should the opportunity present itself, whereas Sarah became ever more determined. They had always had their little signals between them and more than once every day, Sarah would send silently to Sophie:

"Now?" and Sophie would shake her head and nod, perhaps to Lady Penelope or to His Lordship, if he happened to be present, as being reason enough not to try. Although Lord Dalby had come to know them at the same time he had become acquainted with their sister Pennie, he had never seemed to have experienced the least difficulty in telling them apart. They were assured of his love, but they had to assume he was an ally of their sister and so was not to be trusted any more than she.

Of course they did not have much time to brood about the business, for they were much too busy with matters of the greatest importance, namely, their coming out into society, the very reason for their having been brought to London in the first place.

Lady Penelope had had a modest coming out in London many years before her marriage to Lord Dalby, and it had been brought home to her that the daughter of a circuit judge, however excellent her blood, had very little choice in the way of marriage partners. Now that Fate had smiled upon her so bountifully, she was in a situation to see that her sisters would have a better turn at it than she had had. Lord Dalby was just as determined as was his wife. He not only bore the twins great affection and was forever charmed by their antics— why not, the little imps had made it possible for him to gain his lady—but he, too had been but a commoner before he had fallen heir to the earldom. As he was a lawyer of standing in the city, he was quite familiar with the ways of the fashionable world and had every wish to support his wife in favor of his sisters-in-law.

With such enthusiastic sponsorship the twins' plunge into the social whirl of a season now well begun was quite spectacular. The countess held innumerable parties for them at the house in Cavendish Square, and were they dinner parties or balls, still the press of guests was so great that the affairs, one and all, became mere routs. Her Ladyship tried diligently to restrict the guest lists to something manageable but to no avail. There were always friends of friends and relatives of friends, to say nothing of a rich assortment of indigenous, highly eligible, young gentlemen whose stubborn persistence could not be ignored.

Nor was it much different when the twins accepted invitations to other parties. Each hostess, once she had received their acceptance, noised it quickly about to insure that her affair would be behind no others in the number of guests she had garnered.

Only at the more formal and restricted events and places was there any chance for Sophie and Sarah to be able to enjoy themselves without being thoroughly overwhelmed by the attention they were receiving. After some weeks, attendance at Almack's became for them so usual an event that the hallowed place lost all of its awe for them, and their irrepressible charm so enchanted the great ladies who ruled its precincts that they were given permission, much to the delight of the gentlemen attending, to join in the waltz before many another debutante of more advanced age.

Within weeks of Lord and Lady Dalby's introduction to the Royal Court, they, too, were granted an audience. In fact, it was more of a demand than a grant from Her Royal Highness, who had heard so much of the beautiful twins currently taking the town by storm.

In all of this, of course, Lord Blessingame and Lord Fallon, together with Messrs. Deverill and Grantford, had parts to play, but they were very minor roles indeed. They were completely outshadowed by personages of great wealth and greater station, young men, sons of earls and dukes, who came to pay their respects out of curiosity, and stayed, enslaved and enchanted by the vivacious beauties.

Although the twins were quite used to such flattering attentions, that is not to say that it did not go to their heads, and they began to make demands of those admirers they had subjugated—and they were more than a few.

The countess, busily engaged as she was with her own entry into the world of fashion, did not miss the changes that were occurring, and she was not happy about it.

One day she had her sisters sent for. They did not come but sent back that they were going out and would see her when they got back. Lady Penelope, her eyes bright with anger, came after them herself. They were just leaving their room when she came up with them.

"Young ladies, you will march right back into your rooms and sit yourselves down. We are going to have a talk."

"But, Pennie, we are just about to join with Lord Ashton and Lord Vincent for a drive in the park—"

"No, you are not! I have sent your regrets to the gentlemen and they are gone. So you see we shall have plenty of time to come to an understanding."

Sophie and Sarah frowned and would have made an argument, but Her Ladyship said in a quiet voice that they had long learned to respect: "Sophie. Sarah. Pray heed me."

Unconsciously and in unison, Sophie and Sarah trooped back into their room and sat down upon the bed, their hands clasped in their laps, very prim, staring wide-eyed at their sister.

Lady Penelope pulled up a rocking chair and sat down facing them.

"I have been meaning to have a talk with you this past week, and it appears that now is more than time. Sophie. Sarah. You have got to remember that this is not Leicestershire. There things were different. Everywhere you turned you always found yourself amongst friends, people who had known you as children. It is quite the other way about here in London where everyone is a stranger. You do not seem to realize that what goes for cute in our neighborhood back home, in London borders upon the outrageous. Now, you have been carrying about with a decidedly high hand, you are taking it upon yourselves to encourage the attentions of various gentlemen at a whim and without my advice and consent. Alan is more than a little troubled by your goings-on and so am I. You know very well that if Papa and Mama had not returned to Woodhouse, you'd have had a severe talking-to ere this. Unfortunately, my time is too much taken up with the business of being a countess and my husband's wife for me to give proper supervision to you. It grieves me much not to be able to keep you with me, for you know how much I love you, but I fear the time has come for you ladies to remove yourselves to Aunt Claudia's where you can be properly looked after—"

"Oh, Pennie, no! We will give you our word to be more circumspect in the future," exclaimed Sarah, earnestly.

"My dear, it just will not do," replied Lady Penelope. "I have not the time to spare for you— and what is more, Aunt Claudia is far better equipped than I am to counsel a young lady in the decorum that is required in the city. Furthermore, she is dying to have you come to her and has all the time in the world to devote to you."

"But we shall miss all the grand parties, and no gentlemen will come calling—"

"Nonsense! You will miss nothing! Aunt Claudia's is something closer than John o' Groats, child. It is but a long walk from here and nothing so terrible, as you will see. Actually it is a shame that you have not called upon her in all the time you have been in London. Yes, yes, I know there have not been hours enough in the day to do all that we have had to do—but the thing is that I am having to be with Alan and there are no great social functions attending upon your coming out. Now, it is for you to enjoy the rest of the season and avoid giving worry to your family."

"But, Pennie—"

"No, Sarah, there is no use debating the point. You must have the guidance and the protection of an older and wiser female than myself. I am hardly less green than you when it comes to the ways of London, but I am a married woman and that, my dears, makes for a bit of difference. Now, you have been going about with all manner of gentlemen and alone—"

"Oh, but Pennie, you are not being just!" protested Sophie. "It was never *all* manner of gentlemen but mostly Lord Fallon, and Sarah and I were never parted."

"Yes, and that but barely saves your reputations. My sweets, you are gaining a reputation for being quite fast and we cannot permit that to continue. What you must come to understand is that this *is not* Leicestershire! What goes for the district back home just will not do for London. So little a thing as going about the town there is monstrously different here in the city. Sarah, I am sure you must appreciate what I am saying. *You* already have been subjected to a most unsavory experience."

"Oh, I am sure you are making too much of it,

Pennie. Lord Blessingame has made the sweetest apology and—"

"That is not the point, young lady. Just suppose it was not as fine a gentleman as His Lordship who had approached you. No, there can be no question of your going about as you have been doing. There has got to be a responsible female with you and Aunt Claudia is perfectly suited to it—"

"Now, Pennie," began Sophie, storm signals beginning to appear in her eyes.

"Sophie, it is no use your remonstrating with me. You will go to Aunt Claudia's and you will do as she says. You will be guided by her in all things and, if you should insist upon being unruly, you shall have me to answer to immediately—and Mama when I have packed you off to home. I have tried to show you the necessity for it, and since I know that you are not at all slow in the wit department, all this further discussion is but an attempt by you to sway me. Well, because I have become a countess is no reason for believing that you can come it over on me," she said sternly and paused. Then she grinned and added: "Not most of the time, anyway."

The twins sighed.

Sarah asked: "When must we go to Aunt Claudia's?"

"Tomorrow, you will go to pay a formal call upon her with me, and she and you will decide—but I reserve the right to make the arrangements if I do not find yours satisfactory. Now I bid you be of good cheer. It is never so bad as you are making it out to be."

"What about our gentlemen callers, Pennie? Shall we never see any of them again?"

"Of course you shall. It is just that Aunt Claudia will have something to say about whom and when. There can be no objection to Oliver and Percy, of course, and—"

Sarah looked displeased and Sophie sniffed her disdain.

"Great heavens, girls, what has come over you?" exclaimed Lady Penelope. "What can you have to say against either of them?"

They each shrugged and said: "Nothing."

Her Ladyship shook her head and said: "Well, I am not about to say that you have got to see them—but they are both of them upstanding chaps when they are not about you two and it would not hurt you to continue to be civil to them, for they *are* our neighbors and actually the only true friends you have got in London."

"Well, yes, of course, but what about Lord Fallon?" demanded Sophie.

"He is most unexceptional, and if it continues to be his pleasure to call upon you, then you will see him—but he, too, has shown a lack of judgment that I find most disconcerting in a gentleman of his reputation. He ought to have known better than to have taken you up into his curricle for a spin about Hyde Park. He is as much to blame for the talk about you as anyone.

"Now, I shall tell you something to gladden your

hearts and make all of this less burdensome upon you. Alan has received a number of requests from some very eligible gentlemen to speak to you—"

The twins, their faces lighted up with glee, leaped to their feet and rushed over to their sister demanding the names.

Lady Penelope laughed and put them off. "It is early days yet, my dears, to make any difference who they are. As Alan has not the right, he is referring all of such matters to Papa for his approval. Nonetheless, neither of you are to be in any rush about this business. It will be years yet before you would find yourself on the shelf and *that* prospect is inconceivable, I am sure. Do you but enjoy yourselves for this season and leave such heavy matters to the future. You are here to get some bronzing so you shall know how to behave yourselves as fashionable ladies, ladies that the Earl of Dalby and his lady can be proud to call sisters— not to say what we would have Mama and Papa think of you."

"Yes, Pennie," agreed the girls.

"There's my pets," said Lady Penelope smiling.

Aunt Claudia turned out to be a sprightly spinster with a very marked resemblance to her sister Mrs. Sandringham, and the twins, observing how much like their mother their aunt was, were immediately at home with her. As for Miss Dampier, she was delighted to see them and freely expressed her enthusiasm for their coming to join her.

"Oh, how very precious!" she exclaimed. "I do

declare there never were such two perfect darlings!
My, how they have grown. I am sure they could
not have been more than three the last time I saw
them. Oh, what dears! But, Pennie, how in the
world does one tell them apart? Here you have introduced them to me and already I cannot distinguish Sophie from Sarah. I am sure I shall be at it
for ages trying to make up my mind!"

"I would suggest, Aunt Claudia, that for a while,
Sophie wear a bit of pink ribbon and Sarah blue,"
said Lady Penelope. "It will be no time at all before you are quite at ease upon that score."

The twins, standing hand-in-hand, smiled and
said nothing, but Sarah squeezed Sophie's hand in
signal that here was something to their advantage.
Sophie's smile faded a little as she understood that
Sarah saw it as an opportunity to initiate the plan
they had not been able to carry out under Pennie's
eyes.

Her Ladyship left shortly and Aunt Claudia began to take the twins about the house, explain-
ing each room in more detail than the twins cared
to hear.

It seemed that Aunt Claudia's house occupied a
most important place in her life, one that was filled
with visitors of every degree of distinction for
whose reception the dear little house served as a
sort of subordinate hostess. Therefore each room
was filled with mementos of the great and the near
great who had the great good fortune to have
dropped in on Aunt Claudia. Even as she rambled
on about who had sat in which chair and who had

complimented which piece of porcelain, the twins were set to wondering why their aunt should have been so favored. They had never heard anything said in the family that Aunt Claudia was noteworthy beyond the fact that she was the Sandringham's London relation.

The tour could not go on forever, for it was not so big a house to begin with. In fact, it was rather narrower than was common in the city and insignificant by comparison to the Desfords' house in Cavendish Square, so it was not surprising that the room Aunt Claudia announced as theirs was something smaller than what they had been used to. Sophie was about to raise an objection when Aunt Claudia went on to say: "And you can keep your things in the room next door. I have not used it for years and you may have it for a sitting room or whatever. Hmmmm, it is too bad that there is no connecting door, for it would make a cozy apartment for you two girls—and I should not worry about the expense of having one cut except that I do not think you will be with me for so very long. Of course, if you think it is necessary, I shall have it seen to at once."

"Thank you, Aunt Claudia, but, indeed, it would be a needless expense. Sophie and I will be most comfortable here."

"Well, then, I shall have your things brought up. Do you make yourselves comfortable and come down to me in the parlor when you are done. I am dying to have a coze with you. I am sure that you must have unnumbered beaus and I dearly wish to hear all about them. Yes, I do think the dear little house will be coming alive again in the not too distant future," she ended and, conferring a wink upon them, she left them to themselves.

Sophie dropped down upon the bed and bounced up and down on it for a bit.

"Well, we shall sleep well enough. I do declare Aunt Claudia is not the least bit stingy with down."

"Do you believe her when she claims to have entertained all those important people? I do declare I am not familiar with a half of all those she mentioned, but some of them even a dunce must have heard of."

"What does it matter, Sarah dear? If such do call, we shall have the privilege of their company. If not, we shall have the privilege of our own company—and without Pennie or Mama forever clucking about us."

"Yes, and that brings us to the point, I think. Now we can get on with it. I mean to say that if Aunt Claudia cannot tell us apart, we can get on with our little plot. In the meantime we must be particularly careful not to give ourselves away to her."

Sophie frowned. "What ever are you talking about? Why should we have to worry about Aunt Claudia? It will be weeks before she can distinguish between us, I am sure."

"Well, we have got to be sure that she is *never* sure, you stupid goose! At least until we have found out what we wish to know. I say that we each of us should respond to her no matter how she calls us. In that way, she will never know to whom she is speaking even though she will think she does. It will allow us perfect freedom to be each other whenever it pleases us. I think, too, we should take especial pains to see that we do dress exactly alike to maintain the dear lady's confusion."

"Well, we have always done so for as long as I can remember, Sarah. Still, I am not sure that I like the business a bit more than I have ever done. It smacks too much of out and out deceit."

"Oh, for heaven's sake, it is not a whit different from the tricks we played upon the merchants in Loughborough."

"Yes, but we are now something older, methinks. It is time for us to act like ladies and not like hoydens."

"I assure you there is nothing hoydenish in it. One has to be sure that one is at least as smart as the one one has set one's—er, interest—"

"Sarah Sandringham, are you saying that you and Percy—Percy and you—"

"I am not saying anything of the sort! Of course I like Percy. I like him just as much as you like Oliver—"

"Well, I like Oliver as a friend from childhood and that is all. If you had someone like Lord Fallon in attendance upon you, I am sure that Percy would be of no more importance to you than that either!"

"Well, I do! Lord Blessingame is quite the equal of Lord Fallon I am sure."

"Then why do you persist in trying to find out if Percy recognizes you? I cannot care less which of us Oliver thinks I am."

"You cannot mean it!"

"I do mean it! Oliver cannot hold a candle to Lord Fallon!"

"Sophie, you are being quite mean about it! Well, I do not care! I shall be you or I shall be myself as it pleases me. You do what you will and I do not give a fig for the embarrassment it may cause. You had best play along with me if you know what is good for you."

"Now it is you who are being mean, Sarah! You will only succeed in ruining my chances with Lord Fallon, and it will never make a bit of difference to Percy, for he is not quite right in the attic, don't you know."

"You leave my Percy out of it! I admit that there are times when he is not the brightest light in the world, but he always means well. Besides, even as a boy he was most gentle and obliging—more so than Oliver, I must say."

"Oh, now, do not put Oliver down like that! He always means well, too. It is just that he gets himself in a tangle because he does not stop to think but plunges on headlong."

"For heaven's sake, why do you defend him? I thought that he means nothing to you."

"I never said that! I did say that he is a friend from our childhood and I have nothing but good thoughts for him. I mean to say that I can have a good thought about a friend from childhood, can I not?"

"Well, that is what I have a wish to find out, my dear—just how good a friend to us either of them was. I mean to say that if they have been pulling the wool over our eyes for all of this time, then they could not have been such good friends, now, could they?"

"Oh, I think that you are making too much of it. Really, it does not concern me at all."

"Well, it concerns me, and I warn you that I am going on with it. You do as you please."

"Hmph! You give me no choice. Very well—but for how long must we be playing at it?"

"It all depends. I cannot say. Until we can be sure, I dare say."

"Well, I shall not be happy about it."

"For heaven's sake, Sophie, do you think that I am?"

Chapter XI

———◆———

During the days that followed, Aunt Claudia began to go about her little house elated beyond measure. Never before had it experienced such an influx of callers. Thanks to her two delightful relations, it was as if the most select young gentlemen of London were intent upon beating a path to her door. Not only that, there were quite a few ladies in attendance as well. Such connections as the Sandringham twins could boast were an attraction not to be overlooked by matrons anxious to see their male offspring leave off sowing their wild oats and settle down with a wife of distinction; so it behove them to cultivate Aunt Claudia and to bring their daughters along, too, since the Sandringhams could not marry all of the gentlemen they attracted. There was bound to be quite a few of them left over.

There was a constant traffic of carriages on the little street where Aunt Claudia resided, and an extra watchman had to be stationed there by the local constabulary or the thoroughfare would have been blocked solid.

In the house itself, day after day, there was always present more than a few callers, idling about until it became their turn for an audience with Sophie and Sarah. True, undoubtedly many of them came to satisfy their curiosity, others to settle wagers made upon the chances of distinguishing one twin from the other, but mainly, the gentlemen came, at the very least, to get their name down for some future dance with one or the other of the twins. Of them all, there were but four gentlemen who were seriously engaged in trying to get to know the twins as distinct and separate ladies: Oliver and Percy and the lords Blessingame and Fallon.

"Whew! What a damnation crush!" exclaimed Lord Blessingame as he and Lord Fallon stepped into the street. "How the devil shall we make the least progress with the ladies with every bachelor of England underfoot?"

"Oh, I would not concern myself with them. We have got the inside track of all of them, I think. After all we have known the ladies longest and are in a better position to make them out than anybody, I'll wager. That must count heavily in our favor."

"You are forgetting the two lads from Leicestershire, Frank. They have got us on the hip on both scores."

"Yes, but you must consider that for all the advantage that they do have, they do not appear to be in any better suite, with the ladies than anybody else. I take that to mean that they do not stand a chance, or they would have made more of it than they have. In any case, what is there to fear from a Leicestershireman when we are Londoners, born and bred?"

"Aye, there is something in what you say, but I should feel better about it if we were not still so deep in a fog about the ladies' identities. I swear they seem to grow more like each other with every passing day. You know, old chap, it is the damnedest thing, but Miss Dampier does not seem to have the least difficulty with them and I have it on good authority that she has not seen the young ladies since they were mere tots. It is a most discouraging thing! Each time I think I have finally got them sorted out, Miss Dampier will address one of them, and skewer me if she does not say 'Sarah' to the twin I'd have taken my oath was Sophie!"

As they strolled along, Lord Fallon turned a strained look upon his companion and said: "So that has been bothering you, too?" He shook his head and went on: "Indeed, I find it most disheartening. I had thought I was a long way to knowing Sophie from Sarah, but I am confounded at almost every turn. Miss Dampier never mistakes them and like as not I do just about every other chance.

We still are quite a ways from addressing them by their Christian names I fear."

"Quite—which puts us in the same boat with all the rest, for all that we have known them longer. It is my opinion that Grantford and Deverill were particularly ungracious to us to withhold their secret. After all we were quite willing to confer our friendship upon them."

Lord Fallon laughed sarcastically. "Would you have been any more gracious than they if you were in their shoes?"

Lord Blessingame smiled and shook his head. "No, blast them!"

Both Oliver and Percy stood, very ill at ease, before His Lordship, the Earl of Dalby. He was seated behind his desk high with court documents, idly toying with a pen as he gazed at the two young gentlemen, a slight smile of amusement on his lips.

Oliver shifted his feet and glanced at Percy. Percy frowned and motioned at him to proceed.

"It is a bit sticky, this," said Oliver. "I am always the one who has had to speak for us. Why do you not go ahead for once."

"Because I do not know what I am to say. I have never done anything like this before, you idiot."

"Well, you imbecile, neither have I!"

"Oliver, are you sure you want to go through with it? I mean to say, are you sure you can tell Sophie from Sarah?"

"Yes, dammit! I am sure! I told you I could, didn't I? I understand what it was that made the difficulty. I was trying too hard—and that is why you could not explain it to me. It's a feeling that you have about them. It is not anything in particular. If you just ease off a bit and let yourself feel, if you understand me, it comes to you in a flash— and you know directly whether it is Sophie or Sarah. Now, there's a good chap. Speak to His Lordship!"

"Well, if you are sure you know what you are doing, all right," responded Percy. He turned to the earl.

"My lord, I respectfully request for my friend Oliver Grantford and myself Percy Deverill your permission to address ourselves to your sisters-in-law the Misses Sandringham. You see the way it is, my lord, Sarah is mine and Sophie is Oliver's."

His Lordship chuckled and said: "Bravely spoken, Mr. Deverill. I do believe you have covered the ground thoroughly— But what do I hear? Is it a fact that Mr. Grantford, after all the years he has known the twins, still is uncertain as to which is which?"

"Oh, my lord, it is not to be wondered at. I have had the same difficulty—but it has only been recently that it has come a matter of importance to us. You see, it would be a devilish go if we could not recognize our own wives. A most confusing bit of business, don't you think?"

"Indeed, I do! I most certainly do!" said his Lordship, laughing out loud.

Percy grinned. "Yes, it is rather comical—but I do not think the twins would have found it so. Fortunately, once we had to give it serious thought, we were able to do the trick. Now we are quite confident that we have got them pinned down."

"Well, I certainly hope so. I should hate to think what Sophie and Sarah would have to say to it if you proposed to the wrong young lady."

Said Oliver, a pained expression on his face: "My lord, I wish you would not even mention it. It is rough enough on a chap to have to pop the question—but to the wrong lady? It is enough to turn one's knees to water, I do assure you, my lord."

His Lordship, still smiling, shook his head doubtfully. "Well, I wish you all the luck with your respective ladies. Indeed I do—but I am not the person you have to speak to. Athough Sophie and Sarah enjoy my protection, yet are they in the hands of His Honor, Judge Sandringham. I respectfully submit that it is the Judge, their father, to whom you must turn at this juncture."

"But, my lord," said Percy, "His Honor is on circuit in Leicestershire and cannot be conveniently reached. I venture to say, with all due respect, that Judge Sandringham would not have the least objection to your standing in for him. As you are an earl and a judge yourself, with the ladies under your protection, it makes a deal of sense that you act for His Honor in this matter."

"And pray just what is your rush, Mr. Deverill? You can reach His Honor with an express in a matter of a day or so. Within three days, you will have his permission, I am sure."

"Since you are sure, my lord, why must we wait those three days?"

"Because that is how it is done. If the father is living, he has the say."

"And, my lord, if—just supposing, of course— His Honor was not, then what?"

"Why then, I suppose, it would be my duty."

"Now, my lord, I beg your indulgence for a moment. I would sum it up for you. All that you have said, it appears to me, is that there is no objection to Oliver and myself speaking to the ladies. It is merely a matter of form. Well, I put it to you, Your Honor, would it not be a fact that His Honor, Judge Sandringham, would never think to reverse your decision in this matter, regardless of the breach of form?"

The earl blinked and peered hard at Percy. A thoughtful look settled on his countenance as he regarded the young gentleman. "I say, Percy, have you ever considered the law as an avocation? I am looking about for a clerk at this very moment."

Percy beamed. "As a matter of fact, I have, my lord." His smile faded and he shook his head. "But the governor will not see it. He says I shall have all that I can manage, just filling his shoes. He's a viscount, you know."

"Good lord, what has that to say to anything? I am an earl and a judge. What if I were to send a note to the viscount in this regard?"

"Oh, my lord, would you? It could make all the difference!" cried Percy.

"What the devil!"exclaimed Oliver. "You never said a word to me on the subject!"

"What was the use? You would have just jeered at me."

"Did you ever say anything to Sarah about it?"

"No, why should I have? My lord, my father, would not hear of it. Why talk of it?"

"Well, dammit, Percy, what am I to do while you pretend to be His Lordship's clerk?"

"For heaven's sake, Oliver, there always has been something for you to do!"

"Oh, yes, and pray what is that?"

"Your father shan't live forever, you know. You shall have to manage his estate eventually. What is the objection to your assisting him in that endeavor right now? You know, Oliver, you have got to consider that here we are, about to ask the ladies we love to be our wives, and we are both of us but mere pensioners of our fathers. I say if ever there was a time for us to grow up and face responsibility, it is now."

"Hear, hear!" shouted the earl, clapping his hands together in approval. "Very well spoken, my lad! I think I have found me my clerk, by God!"

Percy bowed while Oliver looked thoughtful.

Finally he nodded and said: "Old chum, there is no denying you are right—but the thing of it is it will call for separation of the twins. You know they have never been apart. How do you think they will take it, Sophie with me in Leicestershire and Sarah here in London with you?"

Percy's face dropped as he exclaimed in a hoarse voice: "Great Scot! I never thought of that!"

"Methinks you chaps are putting the cart before the horse," suggested the earl. "It might well be that the ladies would have a word or two to say to it—and the word may be good."

"Do you really think so, my lord?" asked Percy earnestly.

"Far be it from me to think anything about it, lad—but, truly, you have no choice but to put it to your lady. I should be an utter fool to think that I can predict a lady's thoughts upon any topic."

"Then I take it, my lord, that you will allow Oliver and me to approach the ladies on this matter?"

The earl smiled and nodded. "Yes, you have made your point in a most excellent fashion, and my curiosity is aroused to an infinite degree. I shall be all impatience to know how Sophie and Sarah decide."

"Thank you, my lord," said Percy, bowing.

"Your most grateful servant, my lord," said Oliver, very seriously, doing the same.

They turned and left the office.

The smile lingered on the earl's lips as he stared at the doorway.

"It is truly amazing, but you never can tell what is in a man until a woman enters the picture."

"Now what do we do?" asked Percy as they

made their way out of the house. "Pop the question?"

"No, you ass! Surely we can manage something more graceful than that. Er—I am not exactly sure at the moment, however."

"Now, look you, Oliver, I did the business with the earl. It is your turn now. It was always you before this who took the helm, so to speak."

"I pray you will let me be for a moment. Blast you, you have started me thinking and that is an exercise I am not used to."

"What is there to think about? You are in love with Sophie, are you not?"

"Well, of course I am! It is nothing new to me. The thing is the day has come and I am not all that sure that I am prepared to meet it, don't you see. Suddenly, matters have turned serious for me and you have been not the least help."

"For heaven's sake, how do I come into it?"

"You have stolen a march on me, my boon companion; that is how! Why did you not tell me of your plans? It would have put me on notice. Now, here you are, all primed to make an offer, and you do have something to offer; whereas I have not a thing to say to Sophie—and I am not all that sure that I shall recognize her either!"

"But you just told Lord Dalby—"

"Well, dammit, before His Lordship I had to say something more than I felt or what sort of a case would I have had?"

"But you said it just right, for that is precisely how it is with me. It is never a question of a detail of a feature or of dress or mannerism, it is just that I know it is Sarah when I am speaking to her. It just is nothing you have to think about. You just know it."

Oliver appeared to be slightly encouraged. "I say, you are not bamming me just to give me heart?"

"Well, of course I am trying to give you heart, but I am not lying to you."

"I am very much encouraged. Now it is the other business that has me unsettled."

"What business?"

"How we are to go on. I mean to say, you have got a title coming to you eventually. That must say a lot in your behalf."

"Oh, for God's sake man, the twins are not about to be influenced by any such consideration and you know it!" protested Percy.

Oliver sighed. "Yes, that is true. I dare say I am being a bit of a fool."

"A coward more like. Come, Oliver, step to the mark and brace up, old chap."

"Oh, you can say that easily enough. You have no Lord Fallon to contend with."

"Oliver, what has come over you? You are sniveling! Let me put it to you this way. You have got to declare yourself to Sophie and take what comes. If it is not to be, you had best know it now or you will continue to live in a fool's paradise. I think better of Sophie than that. I think that she has got stars in her eyes over this Fallon fellow and it is up to you to bring her down to earth and into your arms."

Oliver stared at his friend in amazement. "You know, Percy, I am beginning to think that for all that we are such close friends, I never truly came to know you. Have you changed, or is it that I have missed something in you?"

"I do not know what you are talking about, but the fact of the matter is that it has come to me Sarah is the only thing that matters to me and I have got to speak my piece—and it has got to be the best that I am capable of. Do not think that I am not in a sweat over it. I have Blessingame in *my* hair, and Sarah is not discouraging the gentleman, from what I have been noticing."

"All right, Percy, I shall put a good face upon it—at least as good as you do—and we shall beard the ladies in their den."

Percy conferred a look of pain upon Oliver. "Really, old chap, that is hardly a pleasant way of putting it."

When Sarah learned that Alan had offered a clerkship to Percy, it gave her something of a turn. She had always had a spot of affection for Percy, perhaps even something warmer than what she felt for Oliver; but she never thought of him as being anything but—Percy, a very nice young man with whom she had spent many hours of her childhood, an amusing boy who was more witless than witty and, therefore, amusing in a touching sort of way. To be clerk to a King's Bench judge must speak loudly to the fact that there was a deal more substance to the young man then she could ever have imagined. Coming, as she did, from a family on intimate terms with the judiciary, she did not need her father to tell her that Percy was now a gentleman of great promise. It also brought her back to the question of just how clever Percy truly was.

More than before, she was now determined to test him. She did not stop to decipher the puzzling mood she was in concerning him. She had been sure she knew Percy better than did his mother and she was bound to find out if this was so.

Sophie, when she heard the news, was surprised, too. Her opinion of Percy was much the same as her sister's but reinforced by never being able to recall a time when Percy was the spokesman for Oliver and himself. It had always been Oliver who led and always, it seemed to her, Percy who followed. To see Percy suddenly elevated over Oliver struck her as being grossly unfair and she might have had a thing or two to say to it except that it could hardly be any of her business. Nevertheless, she discovered herself more willing than before to lend herself to Sarah's scheme. For the sake of their childhood friendship, she owed it to him to prove him superior to the forever befuddled Percy. If Alan was to do so much for Percy, there was every reason for him to do at least as much for Oliver.

So it was that when Sarah said the time was come for them to put their little plot in action, Sophie replied: "Yes, it is time."

Sarah regarded her sister with surprise. "I did not think I should have such an easy time with you, my dear."

"It is only that I have come to think that Oliver is definitely a superior person as compared to Percy and would see it established."

"How very odd! I do not recall that I ever claimed there was all that much difference between them."

"Well, I see a distinct difference and it is all in Oliver's favor. It seems to me that Alan is being quite unfair, making Percy his clerk and never giving any consideration at all to Oliver's fine qualities."

"But, Sophie, Alan was not making a choice between them. It was only that he was impressed with the way Percy could marshal the facts of a case and present them convincingly. He said as much, and it turns out that Percy has always had a liking for the law. He never had any great hopes in that regard because his father was dead set against it. You heard Alan say so."

"Yes, and never a word as to Oliver. It was all Percy, Percy, Percy!"

"Good heavens, sister, what has come over you? If I did not know how taken you were with Lord Fallon, I could swear that you had more than a tendre for Oliver."

"Well, it is hardly anything like that. I just do not wish to see Percy put over Oliver. It is not just!"

"And you think that we can test them with this scheme to prove something?"

"Yes. It will certainly show you how clever Oliver is and that will be a beginning."

"A beginning for what, may I ask?"

"Sarah, now don't you go making too much of it. Just because you are sweet on Percy is no reason that I have to be sweet on Oliver."

Sarah frowned. "I do believe that you put my interest in Percy too strongly. My purpose in this venture is nothing more than to determine if either of them or both have been coming it over on us all these years."

"So you have said and I do not believe you for an instant."

"If it comes to that, sister dear, know then that I do not believe you, either," retorted Sarah, her lower lip starting to quiver.

Sophie's lip was quivering, too. Suddenly they were in each other's arms weeping copiously upon each other's shoulder.

As the sobs subsided, torrents of apologies displaced the tears, followed by declarations of undying affection; and so they were able to resume the thread of their conversation without further comments upon the degrees of enthusiasm their scheme engendered.

Said Sarah: "I think that the best time for it is when neither Alan nor Pennie are about. Aunt Claudia is a dear, but she cannot tell us one from the other if her life depended upon it."

"And it must be when we are apart from each

other so that they have got to really know us.
Then, if they do, we can be sure."

"And I think that as long as we are about it
Lord Blessingame and Lord Fallon should not be
exempt from the business."

Surprisingly enough Sophie agreed without de-
mur.

"Now, then, when shall it be?" asked Sarah.

"Almack's?" suggested Sophie.

"No, Pennie is bound to come along to see that
we are behaving like perfect ladies. I must admit it
makes of Almack's a bit of a bore."

"Too true. Well, then, we shall just have to wait
for an affair which neither Pennie nor Allen can
attend."

"I have got it!" exclaimed Sarah. "Lady Haversham's. We are going with Aunt Claudia because
Lord and Lady Dalby have to attend Lord Ellenborough's dry-as-dust dinner party for notables in
the profession."

"Yes, of course. I am sure that everyone else will
be at the Havershams'. Now then, precisely how
shall we go about it? The dance cards!"

Sarah frowned in perplexity. "I am not sure that
I follow you. If they put their names down upon
our cards they will know us for sure by the number
of the dance. Surely we must assume they are
bright enough to do that."

Now it was Sophie's turn to frown in thought.
She nodded: "Yes, but it will only make the
business easier, don't you see."

"No, I do not. It appears to me that at the very

least we shall have to arrange it that each gentleman dances with the both of us—"

"No, no, not at all! I shall dance with Oliver and Lord Fallon and you with Percy and Lord Blessingame. If either of our partners appears to recognize us—or assumes that we are whom they think we are—we will just deny it and see how they respond to it. If they truly know which of us is which, they will see it as a joke."

"How very clever! Yes, it is quite the easiest thing. I should have had to spend all evening on the business. Oh, but I say! What if none of them is fooled? What then?"

Sophie shrugged. "I should imagine that it goes to say that our days of playing at tomfoolery are over and done with and we shall not have to worry about the gentlemen we decide upon. They will know us."

"Ah, yes, that would be a relief. I say, Sophie, once this business is over, what say we agree to dress differently? I think this being a twin is becoming a bit of a bore, don't you?"

Chapter XII

———◆———

Since the Havershams' party was still a few days off, Sophie and Sarah took the opportunity to insure that Oliver and Percy got their names down on their dance cards well in advance of the festivities. From their experience at recent affairs they knew how ill at ease were the two young gentlemen at London balls. There was always the crush that developed as soon as the twins made their appearance as most of the unattached males made a boisterous effort to gain a dance with one of the twins. In the bedlam of confusion, neither Oliver nor Percy stood any chance at all. They just were not used to such mad goings-on and did not know how to begin. When it came to balls, Leicestershire affairs were ever so much more sedate than these London crushes.

Early on, both Oliver and Percy made complaint

to Lady Dalby at their lack of success in garnering
dances with their former playmates, and her ladyship, thinking it a shame that they should be so
left out of things, consulted with her sisters. Both
Sophie and Sarah understood the situation and,
from that time on, managed to save a space on
their cards, Sophie reserving a dance for Oliver and
Sarah reserving one for Percy.

Now, in order to carry out their stratagem, it
was necessary to insure that Lord Blessingame and
Lord Fallon were assured of a place on their respective cards. While it was a matter of inconse-
quence where Oliver and Percy were concerned, it
was quite the other way about with Their Lordships. The noble gentlemen were bound to take it
as a special mark of favor if the twins arranged for
a dance with them so early before the party. This
consideration merited discussion.

Sophie and Sarah were seated in their sitting
room. It was after breakfast but before ten o'clock
when they might expect their first callers of the
day.

"Well, now, I am sure that they will be calling
today and we still do not know how to go about
it," said Sarah.

"If we are to succeed in this, we shall just have
to ask them," replied Sophie.

"Oh, but even for us that is too fast," protested
Sarah. "I mean to say, it just is not done. They are
bound to think we are rather sweet on them."

"Speaking for myself, I do not find that so ob-
jectionable concerning Lord Fallon."

"Truly, I do not think you ought to encourage him, Sophie, until you are sure. Remember, this is London, and I have found that the gentlemen here are fast enough as it is. They need very little encouragement, it appears to me."

"I could wish that they would lend a little bit of it to some gentlemen from Leicestershire I wot of."

"Goodness gracious, Sophie, I do wish you would make up your mind! Is it to be Lord Fallon or is it to be Oliver?"

"Oh, how can I say! Lord Fallon's manners are impeccable, and that is a deal more than can be said for Oliver—and, too, His Lordship is always in the best of spirits, whereas Oliver is forever deep in a sulk. I do not see why he ever bothered to come to London in the first place."

"This is not getting us anywhere, pet. Leave Oliver be for a moment and think on how we can be assured that Their Lordships will dance with us."

"We shall just have to ask them."

"Never on your life! Sophie, I know you can be a lot more clever than this. Will you kindly apply yourself?"

"Sarah, it all started as the most simple of anything we ever tried. For some unknown reason, it has become excessively complicated. There are obstacles everywhere we turn. Getting Alan to wed Pennie was so much easier."

"We are only fooling ourselves if we persist in thinking that we had all that much to do with it. You will have to admit that they were in love with each other before we put our fingers into the pie."

"Even so, we are having more than our rightful share of trouble with this one, I do declare."

"Perhaps it is because we are so much more involved with it than we are used to being. After all, as far as you are concerned, it may make up your mind between Oliver and Lord Fallon."

Sophie looked at Sarah for a moment. Then she said: "And you? What is your choice between? I was never impressed that Lord Blessingame was of any interest to you."

"He was not. I am not so fond of the London gentlemen as you. I pray that Percy is a lot smarter than he seems. Truly, Sophie, it would be awful if he actually could not tell us apart. I do not know what I shall do."

Now Sophie was concerned. "Sarah, how can you be so struck with Percy so suddenly? You never said anything to me about it."

"The thing is I never thought about it before. We have been so young and matrimony was always so far off into the future—but, since we have come to London, it is all that people talk about. It gives one to think."

Sophie frowned. "But Percy, when there are so many more eligible than he—and ripe for the plucking, I might add."

Sarah's eyes glinted as she looked at her sister. "You are not so different from me, sister dear. It is only that Lord Fallon is so polished a gentleman that you are blinded to your own heart."

"Oh, pooh! I can say that it is much the same with you, sister dear. If Lord Blessingame was not so awkward with you at the first, you might well be looking at him with an entirely different light in your eyes."

"You know in your heart and soul it goes a lot deeper than that. True, Oliver, of late, has been something less than his usual self, but how will you feel if you have to refuse his offer when he makes it? *If* you can refuse him, that is."

At that moment, a maidservant appeared to inform the ladies that Lord Fallon and Lord Blessingame were inquiring for them.

Since nothing had been resolved by the conversation, neither twin was in a particularly good humor as they left their chambers to descend to the drawing room.

"Shall either of you gentlemen be attending Lady Haversham's party?" asked Sarah, after the usual patter of greeting was got over.

"Only if we may expect that our dear delights will be in attendance, my dear Miss Sandringham," replied Lord Fallon, gallantly.

"Ah, and who may these fortunate ladies be, if I may be so bold as to inquire?" asked Sophie.

"Ah, that would be telling, would it not?" returned Lord Fallon, smiling archly.

Sophie pouted. "Well, since you will be so occupied with your heart's interest, I have suddenly decided that I shall not attend. After all, who would I have left to dance with?"

"Miss Sandringham, I beg you not to change your mind," said Lord Blessingame. "It will be my very great pleasure to see that you have all the dances you desire, even if I have to dance every one with you myself."

Lord Fallon laughed. "Blast you, Jack, if you have not outmaneuvered me! Miss Sandringham, I pray you will not accept my friend's generous offer or I shall be heartbroken."

"Indeed, my lord," said Sarah, "then how could we refuse? But which of us is it you would prefer?"

But His Lordship was not such easy game as all that. He laughed and replied: "Oh, you may be assured that I shall dance with both you lovely ladies before the evening is out, if you will allow it."

Sophie knitted her brows and said, hesitantly: "Well, I do not know if that can possibly be arranged. You must know how it is—we are so much in demand, we may not have room on our cards. Do you not think so, Sarah?"

Sarah gave her a withering look, but then, with a smile, she replied: "Truly, it is difficult to say how it will be. I dare say it will be a matter of first come, first danced with. Do not you think so, Sophie?"

"Ah!" exclaimed Lord Fallon, brightening visibly. "Then I would have you put my name down, my dear Miss Sophie, allowing Lord Blessingame, here, the pleasure of a dance with Miss Sarah."

Replied Sophie, looking quite satisfied: "My lord, I am sure that I speak for my sister as well as myself when I say how pleased we are to accede to your gracious request."

After they were gone, Sarah turned on Sophie. "You gave it all away, you idiot!"

"What was the use? You saw how Lord Fallon was behaving. He was not about to commit himself."

"If that is so, we have no need to regard His Lordship further," said Sarah.

"Of course, he could have been toying with us. We could not be sure he was not. In any case, I shall have a dance with him and then I can make sure of it."

"Lord Blessingame did not have too much to say. He is a quiet sort, and it is rather difficult to tell about him."

"Well, he cannot escape it, no matter how quiet he is. 'Miss Sandringham' just will not do at Lady Haversham's."

"Quite—or they shall have the greatest difficulty trying to explain why they are not on a first-name basis with us. We have managed to bring them forward that far at least."

Said Sophie: "Yes, I think it is going along swimmingly now. The stage is set and we shall quickly learn which of our beaus is the cleverest."

"Cleverest? What in the world is so clever? We are only trying to determine how well acquainted any of them is with us. I shall certainly be glad when it is all over."

"Yes, my dear, it is not proving to be any fun at all."

Chapter XIII

———◆●◆———

Lady Haversham's parties were always well attended, but she used discretion in compiling her guest list so that her affairs never degenerated into mere routs where any pretense at dancing was defeated by the press of people on the dance floor. As a result, the festivities were well ordered, the refreshments never ran out, and everyone generally had a good time.

This evening was no different. As the twins came into the ballroom with Aunt Claudia just behind them, the hum of conversation died away and a general movement of young men in their direction began. In no time at all, both their cards were filled and a great many gentlemen were forced to retire in disappointment. It was obviously going to be a most enjoyable evening for the ladies Sandringham.

Those gentlemen whom fortune had favored with a place on the cards gathered round and a conversation began, filled with frequent sallies and much laughter. Missing from the group were Lords Blessingame and Fallon. They were a little older than the rest and, since they knew that they had their dances reserved, did not deign to join the "juveniles."

"I say, Frank, what the devil was going on that day we called and won the twins' consent to our dancing with them?" asked Lord Blessingame. "I had the distinct feeling that something was up."

"I know what you mean, old chap—and I am beginning to think it was their curiosity."

"Well, now, if it were so, I should take it as a most encouraging sign, wouldn't you?"

"I am not so sure," replied Lord Fallon, screwing up his eyes in thought. "There was the eagerness of the hunt about Miss Sarah that I cannot say I liked very much—you know what I mean. It was as if she were hot on the scent."

Lord Blessingame made a face. "That is hardly a nice way to allude to a lady, don't you know. But what the devil are you saying? It was all perfectly innocent as far as I could see."

"Well, it was not so for us, old thing. As a matter of fact I meant to have a talk with you about it. Where in blazes have you been these past few days?"

"Here and there. I say, Frank, why are you getting your wind up so?"

"Because I think they trapped us, you fool!"

—

"Now just a moment there! Who are you calling a fool?"

"The two of us! Think, man! What is it we have been trying to avoid with them?"

"Oh, bless my soul! I say, do you think they did it on purpose?"

"How the devil should I know. The fact remains that we did address them by their first names and now there is no turning back. We have got to continue to do so!"

"The devil you say!" exclaimed Lord Blessingame, visibly shaken. "But, Frank, old chap, it is not possible! I could not tell them apart this day to save my life?"

"Well, neither can I, blast! I thought that I had got it, following Miss Dampier's lead but, in the end, I was confounded."

"Aye, so you said. Frankly, I got the distinct impression that Miss Dampier was in the same straits with us on that score and that the twins were going along with her just to humor her."

Lord Fallon looked at Lord Blessingame in surprise. "By Jove, I do believe you are right!"

"All cheers and commendations to me, friend, but what good does that conclusion do us? We have still got to dance with them and, if we dance with them, we have got to talk with them, and 'Miss Sandringham' will no longer serve. I am blessed if it will!"

"If only we had had the good sense to have talked this business out between us. Why, in heaven's name, did you pick this time to make yourself so scarce?"

"Oh, I say! Leave off! The fact of the matter is that we are faced with an impending catastrophe and there is no way that I know to avert it. Perhaps we ought to beg off. Illness or some such excuse."

"What, the both of us? Be sensible, Jack!"

"All right, then, one of us. Better one of us be embarrassed than both of us."

"And of course, you are quite prepared to sacrifice your evening in this good cause, leaving me to bear the brunt of the ladies' scorn, I dare say."

Lord Blessingame grinned. "Precisely!"

"Oh, go to blazes!" said Lord Fallon with a laugh. "But the thing that baffles me is the question as to whether or not they did this thing on purpose."

"I suspect we shall get our answer before the evening is much older. The first dance is beginning and we have got to go over there and choose our partners."

"Don't you mean 'claim'?"

"No, by Jupiter! We have got to choose amongst them before we can claim 'em!"

"Well, here's at 'em, lad! What say I take the one on the right?"

"It's as good a choice as any, I suppose. Have at 'em!"

Both Sophie and Sarah were somewhat taken aback by the resoluteness with which their partners came to claim them for the first dance, and more than a little pleased that the gentlemen had chosen rightly. They went off on the arms of Their Lordships in a gay mood. Things might not turn out so disappointing after all.

The dance had been in progress a few minutes when Sarah smiled up into Lord Blessingame's face and said, lightly: "My lord, I'll tell you a secret. I am Sophie."

His Lordship appeared to stumble, and a tide of crimson flooded over his features. He held tightly to her hand and drew her off the floor, staring hard at her as they passed to the side of the great chamber.

Once out of the way of the dancers, he bowed to her and said: "Miss Sophie, I humbly crave forgiveness, but I fear I cannot go on with you. It comes to me that if, after all this time, I am unable to distinguish between you and your sister—and you must know I truly cannot—then embarrassments far greater than this must be my lot in the future. You are charming, Miss Sandringham, you are beautiful, Miss Sandringham, but not a whit more than your sister, Miss Sandringham. It is bad enough that there is not that much difference in your qualities to allow a man to choose between you; but, when you add the hazard that there is naught else to distinguish you, one from the other, I say that is too much for any man. In any case, it is far too much for me. Miss Sandringham, I bid you good evening."

He bowed to her and strolled off, taking out his handkerchief to mop a very troubled brow.

Sarah was filled with conflicting emotions. There was disappointment, but there was also fear. Had she and her sister gone too far with their pranks? Would any man be able to tell one of them from the other? For the moment, the thought that there were those that could mark her from her sister escaped from her consideration, and she felt somewhat stricken as she found herself a seat and sat down.

Dancing with Lord Fallon was a pleasure. Sophie found him exceedingly graceful and very easy to follow. At the same time, he kept her chuckling with his light, airy bantering that demonstrated a wit of high order. The fact that he had been able to distinguish her from Sarah so easily added something of exultation to her happy mood as they went through the figures of the dance.

So it was that she had not the slightest hint of misgiving when she smiled and looked up at him, saying: "My lord, what if I were to tell you that you are dancing with Sarah?"

She saw the smile wiped off his face, and her heart dropped within her, but they continued to dance. She wanted very much to reassure him that, in truth, he had chosen right, to see the smile restored, but it was too late. His whole attitude was suddenly gone stiff and the look of disappointment in his eyes as he stared hard at her told her that there was no going back. He did not know who she was! His next words confirmed her suspicions.

Lord Fallon took a breath, restored his smile and looked down at her. "My dear Miss Whoever-you-are, it has been a most interesting and unusual experience to know you, but you must realize that it is bound to shake up a man to have to admit that the lady he nurses a tendre for is beyond his instant recognition—nor is that the least of the matter. Miss Sandringham, I cannot tell you from your sister and I do not know if I ever shall be able to. One thing I do know, and that is, I am not about to spend the rest of my life worrying at the problem. I pray we may remain friends, but I should be a fool to try for anything more than just that."

Sophie was on the verge of tears for the rest of the dance.

During the intermission for refreshments, Sophie and Sarah were able to get together to compare notes. As they approached each other, their faces were a perfect match to the last detail of the expression of their unhappiness.

"What are we to do?" exclaimed Sarah, clasping hands with Sophie.

Sophie sighed. "We must go through with it no matter how unhappy it makes us. Sarah, it is as Lord Fallon said to me. A gentleman cannot go on forever guessing as to whom his lady is. Oh, Sarah, *must* we go on with it?"

Sarah took hold of Sophie's hands. "You know that we must. Sophie, it has got to be the same for us. We cannot go through life forever wondering if our love truly knows us from each other. I am sure it would make for all kinds of difficulty."

"Oh, but surely, it need not be so. We have already agreed to dress differently and try to change our mannerisms so that we can be more readily distinguished."

"Oh, Sophie, how I wish it were that simple—but it is not. After all, Pennie, Papa, Mama, and Alan, too, have no difficulty at all in telling us apart, and I suspect that it is because they have always loved us. And there are others, too. Not all the world finds it impossible. Surely, that is something we have to demand of any man we may consider for our spouse."

"Well, now, perhaps, we are rushing things. There is Aunt Claudia. She cannot tell us apart, and you dare not say she does not love us. I have lost Lord Fallon and I think it is only because it is just too soon."

Sarah appeared to vacillate. "Perhaps you are right—but it just does not sit well with me. It alarms me the very thought that one I love cannot know for sure it is I. No, Sophie, we have started this and we must go through with it. I cannot believe that, after all these years, Percy does not know me."

"Oh, I do not know what to think! What if Oliver should turn out to be the only man who knows me? Is it he I *must* marry?"

"Truly, Sophie, you surprise me. Indeed, I am sorry to learn that Oliver affects you so little, but he is not the last man on earth. There will be others—and I am sure if we cease to stress our similarity, things will improve. I am sure of it. Still, we ought to go through with it—for my sake if not for yours. I would come to understand Percy better, and this is a way to do it."

Sophie agreed spiritlessly.

Sophie's heart lifted a little as Oliver came toward her. There was a happy light in his eyes as he held out his hand and said: "Oh, Sophie, you cannot know how *delighted* I am to see you!" His tones were positively joyful.

Frowning slightly, Sophie smiled. "Oliver, one would think you had not seen me in a very long time, yet it was but two days ago that you called."

"Nevertheless, my dear, I am truly, truly delighted to see you again. It *is* as though I never saw you before. Come, the music is beginning."

"No, wait. Oliver, before we go out on the floor, tell me one thing. How sure are you that you are speaking to Sophie and not to Sarah?"

Her heart sank as she witnessed all the confidence drain from him. He stared wildly at her and exclaimed: "Oh God! Surely, I cannot have been mistaken. If you are Sarah, then—then . . ."

He could not go on. There was that in his face that tore at the very heart of her, so that she had to clutch at her throat. "Oliver, no—Oliver!"

But it was too late. Clenching his trembling lip between his teeth, he had made a slight bow to her, turned away and walked quickly through the throng and out of her sight.

It was horrible—the pain. Never before had Sophie experienced anything like it. She had hurt Oliver and, when it was too late, came to understand that she had hurt her love and wounded herself grievously at the same time. It was too much emotion to fill one heart, and her tears streamed down her cheeks as she hurried over to the stairs to find herself a place, away from the people enjoying themselves. She needed solitude and she needed time. She needed to think. She needed to weep.

At the head of the stairs she saw a closed door and rushed toward it as though it were some particular haven, regardless of the stares from the other ladies standing about in the hall, gossiping.

She opened the door quickly and slipped inside.

There was Sarah, half reclining on a bed, her eyes as wet as her own.

"Oh, Sarah!" wailed Sophie, holding out her arms.

"Oh, Sophie!" wailed Sarah, holding out her arms.

They came together with a rush and broke down completely, sobbing loudly on each other's shoulder.

They had got their grief and remorse under control and were now sitting on the bed, mopping at their eyes with tear-soaked handkerchiefs.

"How was it between Percy and you?" asked Sophie.

"Awful! Oh, I shall never forget Percy's look when I told him that I was you." She started to sniffle again.

"Please, Sarah," implored Sophie, placing her hand on Sarah's, consolingly.

Sarah looked at her and there was puzzlement in her eyes. "But you? Why are you so affected. Oliver never meant so much to you as Percy does to me."

Sophie bowed her head. "I did not know before. But the way I felt when he appeared so broken before me, it told me all. Oh, Sarah, I do love him and now, because of this foolishness, I have lost him. What am I to do?" She ended with a sob.

Sarah could only shake her head and dab at her eyes again.

They sat together, utterly miserable, neither one with the faintest wish to ever leave the room again.

"He did not say a word!" exclaimed Sarah, suddenly.

"Who?"

"Percy. He just stood there, his face as white as a sheet, transfixed; and my heart broke! Oh, why did I do it! Why did you not stop me!"

But Sophie was busy with her own sad memory of the evening and was not about to respond to her sister's rhetorical questions.

"But we have got to do something, Sarah. I think we ought to seek them out and make our full apologies to them. Beg their forgiveness, too."

"Do you think they could ever forgive us after this? You know we have never been particularly kind to them at any time before. We have always treated them as though they were a little less than bright, if you know what I mean. I suppose that is how I always thought of them. They were so easily managed by us."

"Yes, I suppose it was because they were always in love with us and we took every advantage. Oh, well, now have they got their revenge and with a vengeance!"

"No, Percy is never like that!" protested Sarah.

"No, you are right. I cannot picture Oliver in such a role either. But we must make it up to them, mustn't we?"

"Yes, we must, but how?"

"If it was in the old time, it would have been the easiest thing. They'd have come running if we but beckoned. I dare say it will never be like that again for us."

"No. We felt so clever about it, too. I do not feel very clever, now."

Sophie took a deep breath and sat up straight. "But they do love us!" she declared, trying to draw inspiration from her statement.

Sarah sat up, too. "Yes, and there's a new beginning in it—if only we knew where to start."

"My dear, I fear that there is but one thing left to us. Much as I hate to admit it, we shall have to bring it to Pennie. She is bound to help us—after what we did for her."

Sarah smiled. "You know very well she would help us on any score. Let us go and collect Aunt

Claudia, and tomorrow we shall present ourselves to our sister, the countess."

With that, they finished drying their eyes, inspected each other's appearance and left the chamber to find their aunt.

Chapter XIV

———◆◆◆———

The Earl of Dalby's office, now that he had gained his judgeship, was now dignified by the appellation of His Honor's Chambers at Home, and this morning, he was absent from his bench so that he might devote himself to correspondence that had been piling up on his desk for a week. Alan Desford had always been possessed of a quick mind, and he put it to good use as he riffled through the pile of letters and official documents before him. He was seeking those that called for his immediate attention, putting those aside that were of lesser moment for a later perusal.

He muttered under his breath as the collection of invitations and letters from friends grew to alarming proportions: "Oh, surely Pennie could have culled this lot! Why must I have to do it! She is the countess of the family. Here, what's this!"

He took up the letter which appeared to give him particular offense and reread the sender's name.

"Now what in blazes is wrong with the young cub! Why a letter when he should have been busy at work with me? If he thinks to take advantage of his intimacy with the Sandringhams, the lad is in for a very great surprise."

He unfolded the letter and read it. It was short, formal and to the point.

"Nonsense!" exclaimed His Lordship. He read it again. "Rot!" and reached for the bellrope.

A maid responded and he requested that Her Ladyship attend upon him at once.

As he waited for Lady Penelope, he frowned at the letter, waving it back and forth.

"Yes, Alan, what is it, dear?" asked Lady Penelope as she came into his chamber.

"Here, love, read this and explain it to me, I beg you," he replied, handing the letter to her.

She did not take a seat but stood before his desk as she quickly scanned the sheet. She nodded. "So it has come to this. Poor lad!"

"Poor lad? What about poor Judge! What am I to do for a clerk now that my clerk has tossed his post over without ever having worked at it? What do you mean 'poor lad'?"

Lady Penelope sighed. "I fear, my lord, the twins have outdone themselves this time. They are now with me. They came over this morning, and I have been closeted with them for hours."

A sickly smile crossed the earl's face. "Things

have been too peaceful in their direction. Pray inform me as to what has occurred."

Lady Penelope, the letter still in her hand, sat down and flourished it at her lord and master. "You will not let this silly letter of resignation put you out with Percy, I pray?"

"No, of course I will not. If the twins are involved in it, something strange is always to be suspected."

"Oh, I like that, I do! I do not look upon our marriage as in any way strange—and you will admit that they had something to do with it, my lord," she said, with mock ill-humor.

He laughed. "Oh, do get on with it, my sweet. I have important matters piled up all around me."

"Well, Alan, I think we may rest easy on the score that this must be the last trick that my dear little sisters ever play again. It is a case of the biters being bitten, you see. This time they have been very naughty, indeed, and the punishment has been quick and severe. This is how it happened, so they have told me . . ."

Whatever his annoyance over having to give his attention to such matters, His Lordship showed not a whit less interest. Actually he seemed quite fascinated with the countess' recounting of the twins' disastrous scheme.

He kept a sober mien throughout, but upon her ending the tale, he broke out into hearty laughter.

"Oh, Alan, I am so disappointed in you! How can you be so cruel as to laugh at the sorry plight of my poor sisters?" she asked, sadly, but unable to repress her own chuckles.

She looked at him a great pleading question in her eyes.

He looked back at her and nodded. "I dare say I am supposed to take a hand in this mess."

"Yes, Alan. I fear Papa is too far removed from this sort of business by his age to be able to do anything that will be effective."

"You know, my love, I think I should have married you anyway, if just for the opportunity of observing the doings of those sisters-in-law of mine. I was sure they would never fail to amuse me, and thus far at least, they have not disappointed me. Well, you may leave it to me. I am not about to lose a promising clerk over such a piece of nonsense as this. Leave it to me and do you inform Sophie and Sarah that they had better be on their best behavior from now on or they shall hear all about it from me."

"Alan, you are a dear!" exclaimed Her Ladyship, getting up and going over to him at his desk. Throwing her arms about him and resting her head on his shoulder, she sighed: "Dearest, I am so glad you married me!"

For a moment, the room was stilled with a blissful silence. Finally His Honor disentangled his countess from her seat on his lap and exclaimed: "Enough, you shameless hussy, or I shall never get another thing done this day!"

Two very miserable gentlemen were going about

their chamber, collecting their belongings in a lack-adaisical manner, tossing them, helter-skelter, into their portmanteaus, missing their mark as often as not and not caring a bit.

"I tell you, Oliver, it is not fair! I was so sure! I knew that I was speaking to Sarah. I'd stake my life on it!"

"Yes, old friend, I know exactly the feeling. It was quite the same with me. I cannot understand how I could have been wrong."

"Nothing will convince me that it was not Sarah!" he declared quite angrily. "Ah! I know what it is! Of course, don't you see?"

"No, I do not see. What do *you* see? Not that it can make the least bit of difference to me."

"But it will! Don't you see. She does not love me! That is why she denied she was Sarah! I *was* right all the time!"

Oliver regarded Percy for a moment with pity. "I say, old thing, are you quite sure you have all your pebbles in order? So that makes you happy?"

"No, it does not! What do you think I am? But at least, my mind is all right."

"Well, it's my heart that is giving *me* trouble at the moment. Devil take your mind!"

"Yes, you are so very right. Well, there is nothing left for us to do but to return to Woodhouse, is there."

"I was sure we decided that was the case last night," responded Oliver dryly.

With a boot in each hand, Percy collapsed upon

a sofa loaded with various articles, completely un-mindful of them.

"Oliver, old chap, I have decided. I shall never marry."

"Well, you shall never marry Sarah San-dringham. I'll lay you odds on that."

"Damn it, man, must you make it sound so fi-nal!"

"Percy, you have got to face the fact. If you did know Sarah, then I agree with you. She fooled you because she considers you her dupe, and I am sure no female is going to be in love with one she con-siders so beneath her contempt. On the other hand, if you had mistaken her and it was Sophie you were with, then you do not know your own love and you had best step aside."

"Why must you be so infernally clever at a time like this? You could at least give a chap some hope, you know."

"Unfortunately, dear boy, I am infernally short of that commodity myself. I have none to spare."

There was a knock on the door, and the Boots handed in an official-looking letter.

Percy took it from him and looked a bit shaken. "I say! This has all the appearance of something is-sued by a court. Are we in some sort of trouble?"

"A court? Lawyers and things?"

"Yes," said Percy, grimly, as he worked away at the waxen seal.

He got it open and handed it to Oliver. "Here, you read it. I have no heart for anything at the moment."

"You are too kind," retorted Oliver sourly as he took it and began to read it aloud.

"Hear ye! Hear ye! Know all men by these presents—"

"Oh, give it here! You do not know a thing about the law, do you?"

"I never made claim to!" retorted Oliver.

"Now let me see—Oh, I say! This is awful!"

"What in blazes is the matter?"

"It is something to do with a matter before His Honor."

"Judge Sandringham?"

"No, you dunce! His Lordship!"

"Dalby?"

"Yes!"

"Good God! What have we done?"

"It does not say. It is a summons and we have got to make our appearance before His Lordship, tomorrow at ten in the morning.

"Oh, not at Old Bailey?"

"No, of course not, you idiot. That is for criminals and felons. Naturally it would be at the King's Bench Court— No, it won't! It says it's to be at his chambers in Cavendish Square. Whew! Well, it cannot be all that bad now, can it?"

"I don't know. What do King's Bench judges judge?"

Percy sighed. "They hear cases relating to such things as treason, suppression— Oh, I say, there has got to be some mistake!"

"Well, I would not let it worry you. We have our tickets for the stage. His Lordship will just have to have his hearing without us. We are for Leicestershire."

"Don't be a greater ass than you already are. We shall have to postpone our trip. We cannot fail to make an appearance. Don't you know anything?"

"But Cavendish Square! Suppose we were to meet with Sarah and Sophie. I could not stand it."

"I hardly think they would be present at our trial."

"What trial?" cried Oliver. "We have not done a thing, I tell you."

"I know that and that is what we shall tell the judge. I assure you there is not a thing to worry about. I know something about these matters. Leave everything to me."

"I suppose I must. I say, Percy, do your best, won't you. My governor will not take it lightly, his son in chains."

"Well, we might as well unpack. We have got to stay another day."

Oliver looked about the room. "I cannot say as we have actually packed. The blasted room looks as messy as ever."

Attired in the newest clothes purchased from the finest tailor in London, Oliver and Percy, fighting for every ounce of confidence and self-composure, presented themselves at the house on Cavendish Square at precisely two minutes before ten o'clock. They were admitted at once and led to the earl's office-cum-chambers and announced. They stepped into the room like a pair of martyrs about to be thrown to the lions and stopped dead in their tracks. There did not seem to be anything at all official about the place.

Lady Penelope was seated to one side, and the earl was behind his desk. Across the way were seated two young ladies, each stylishly attired in the latest fashion, the one in pale blue, the other in yellow. Oliver's and Percy's wandering gazes stopped at their faces, and the two gentlemen froze in their tracks.

Why it was Sophie and Sarah and they were not at all alike! That is, the faces were, of course, but that was all.

Lord Dalby waited a moment, observing the little tableau, smiled at his wife and then brought his hand down sharply upon the desk top.

"The court will come to order! I apologize for the absence of a suitable clerk, but you will be pleased to know that I do have one on order. Now then, I, Alan Lord Dalby, by the powers vested in me, etc., have summoned all you present for hearing a case of flagrant breach of identity—"

"Breach of identity?" exclaimed Percy. "I am sure I never heard of such a charge, my lord."

"Come to order, young man! I am sure you never have either, but it will serve us quite well here. The particulars are these: These two young ladies have pleaded guilty to the charge and I am bound to sentence them as it is my duty. Since you gentlemen are a part of their punishment, it is only fitting that you be here to execute the business. As a matter of fact—"

"Your Lordship, I protest!" shouted Percy, stepping bravely forward.

"I do, too!" shouted Oliver, coming forward, too.

"I suggest you gentlemen hold your tongues and listen to the sentence before you disrupt these proceedings again," Lord Dalby said, very sternly.

"Now then, since the point of these proceedings is to establish precisely who is who, it will be up to you to decide. I have it on excellent authority that you, Oliver, and you, Percy, know these ladies. The court would have you prove it. That is sentence."

Oliver regarded the earl in great puzzlement. "I say, Your Lordship, I do not get the point of all this. It is more a punishment to me than anyone else."

Percy added: "For heaven's sake, my lord, we have both of us failed in that direction already, and it was not pleasant, I assure you."

"Oh, Alan, I pray you will not be too hard on them," interposed Lady Penelope.

His Honor looked down his nose at his wife and said. "Your Ladyship, please. Have you no respect for the dignity of this court?"

"I am fast losing what little I did have, Your Honor," she responded with a chuckle.

"Order! Order! Now let us get on with it. Oliver, Percy, I have it on excellent authority that you do *know* the proper identity of these ladies, and so it is up to you to demonstrate to the court the validity of this assertion."

Percy was frowning as he stepped forward. "I

beg your leave, my lord, to ask who is the authority you quote?"

"Why, the ladies themselves, of course, you nitwit!"

Lady Penelope reached for His Lordship's hand in approval as they watched, smilingly, as Oliver and Percy, without the least bit of hesitation, went each directly to his love.

Lady Penelope regarded the colorful huddle in the far corner of the room and said: "My lord, I imagine that this court is adjourned."

He stood up and helped her out of her chair. As they passed from the room, he remarked: "Devil of a business a chap has to go through just to keep a law clerk!"

"Well, at least my sisters will not be able to lord it over you on how they managed to bring us together any longer. I'd say you have just paid them back in full."

"Yes, love, that is a comfort!"

If you have your heart set on Romance, read

Coventry Romances

THE TULIP TREE—Mary Ann Gibbs	50000–4	$1.75
THE HEARTBREAK TRIANGLE —Nora Hampton	50001–2	$1.75
HELENE—Leonora Blythe	50004–7	$1.75
MEGAN—Norma Lee Clark	50005–5	$1.75
DILEMMA IN DUET—Margaret SeBastian	50003–9	$1.75
THE ROMANTIC WIDOW —Mollie Chappell	50013–6	$1.75

*Let Coventry give you
a little old-fashioned romance.*